Mad Martin

Mad Martin

~~~~~~~~~~~~~~~~~~~~~~~~~~~~~~~~~

by PATRICIA WINDSOR

HARPER & ROW, PUBLISHERS
New York, Hagerstown, San Francisco, London

MAD MARTIN

FIRST EDITION

Library of Congress Cataloging in Publication Data

Windsor, Patricia.
  Mad Martin.

  SUMMARY: When his grandfather becomes ill, a silent, solitary boy is taken in by a large foster family where he discovers his own feelings and new ways of relating to others.
  [1. Foster home care—Fiction. 2. Grandfathers—Fiction]   I. Title.
PZ7.W7245Mad   [Fic]   76-3837
ISBN 0-06-026517-5
ISBN 0-06-026518-3 lib. bdg.

To all grandfathers

Chapter 1

〰〰〰〰〰 They lived in the house. It was an ordinary house joined on either side to other ordinary houses, all in a row up and down the London street, all brownish gray brick with three steps up to the front door, net curtains in the front windows. You had to read the numbers carefully to make sure you were going in where you lived and not somebody else's. Sometimes on a sunny Sunday, people came in swank cars to gape and call it quaint.

Mad Martin did not think it was quaint. He didn't think it was much of anything except where he lived, and home. He lived in the house with his grandfather. On the ground floor they had a room and a kitchen. Upstairs they had two rooms, one for him, Mad Martin, and one for his grandfather, Mr. Drivic. Attached to the back of the kitchen was a shed with a sloping roof where there was a cold and clammy toilet. The bathtub was in the kitchen. It had a drain but no taps. When Mad Martin or his grandfather wanted a bath they had to fill it up with pots of hot water. It was an ordeal and mostly they dispensed with it.

In the downstairs front room they had two chairs, a table and a television set. Every evening, Mr. Drivic warmed his feet at the electric fire and snoozed when he watched television. Mad Martin pushed pieces of puzzles under the chairs and his grandfather's feet and made noises while his grandfather snoozed. If he looked up at the television screen he saw things in another world, nothing to do with him. He didn't look often, preferring the games he made with junk on the floor. Sometimes his grandfather stepped on the junk and yelled. Then Mad Martin had to pick everything up and put it away in the box under the table.

Long ago, they had a cat named Shirley but not anymore. Shirley liked to sleep under cars and Mad Martin found her one morning, squashed flat. He looked at Shirley for a long time, wondering if it would be possible to scoop her up and bring her inside. He gave it up as hopeless. His grandfather came out to the street to have a look and said Shirley was now up in the dogs' heaven and not to be bothered by the mess in the gutter as it no longer had a soul and didn't count.

"What's a soul?" Mad Martin wanted to know.

His grandfather, looking tired, took a long while to answer. "A soul is inside a body," he said at last, "the something that thinks and feels, that makes the man what he is. A soul gives life to the body."

This was Mad Martin's first inkling that a thing called a soul lived inside a body and could be let out to escape when the body got squashed. He felt disturbed that Shirley's soul was in a dogs' heaven as Shirley had never liked dogs. He asked his grandfather.

"The mačka will be welcome too," Mr. Drivic said and would explain no more. But it got Mad Martin to thinking about other sorts, like mice and birds and the wild animals he saw in the book in school. He was overwhelmed by the idea of so many different kinds of souls going to special heavens and for a short time he wondered and pondered. He wrote in his diary: "Shirley got squashed and is in dogs' heaven." Then he forgot.

Mad Martin kept a diary faithfully every day. He wrote down everything he did, most of it the same: "I got up. I took in the milk. I ate my cereal. I went to school. I came home. I played. I went to the fish shop for our supper. We ate our supper. I went to bed. I slept." He never added "I slept" until the next morning just in case it would be telling a lie. Also in case he might have an accident in bed and wake up out of his body in the people's heaven, he hoped someone would write "I died" for him so that the diary could be ended and complete.

Occasionally he read through his diary and felt something was missing although he couldn't say exactly what. He had learned about diaries in school when they studied history and the teacher read them a diary by a man called Pepys, pronounced Peeps. It had impressed Mad Martin that a diary was an important thing. He found an old notebook, tore out a few used pages, and began one of his own. But neatly written and daily as it was, Mad Martin's diary seemed to be lacking something. Hard pressed to add importance to the entries, he racked his brains and wrote: "The man at the fish shop gave the wrong change," or "A lady dropped her shopping bag when she got off the bus," but still there was this lingering feeling of dissatisfaction. However, after a time, Mad Martin forgot and went on making his usual daily entries in an untroubled way.

He was quite content. He didn't think he was mad, only Martin. He had no friends because he didn't have them. It did not seem a needful or required thing. No one, in any case, had ever offered or asked to be his friend. Mad Martin did not speak to anyone if he could help it, especially at school. He knew the best routes home in case some of the boys were in a rotten mood. If by chance they caught and thumped him in spite of his circumventions, he nursed his wounds privately and didn't try to understand. He could then add to his diary: "They were in a rotten mood. I have two cuts and a bloody nose." If his grandfather happened to notice cuts or nose, he laughed and shook his head and said, "Boys are always fighting so hard to become men," called him a little junak and didn't ask for any details. Mad Martin sensed that his grandfather thought there was all around mutual kicking and punching in these fights. He never explained to his grandfather how it really was, that it was them doing the punching and him, Mad Martin, getting punched. Once in a while, this bothered him.

But mostly life went along in sameness, seemingly for an eternity, or at least for as long as Mad Martin could remember. He got out of bed every morning as soon as he heard his grandfather's alarm clock ringing. He stepped quickly back into the clothes he had thrown on the floor the night before. He laced his shoes, hoping the many knots wouldn't break again and make the laces too short which would mean searching all over the yard and in the bins for a piece of string or, last resort, trying to get some money to buy new ones. If the knots held it was a good day and he went clamoring down the steep stairs to the front door to get the milk in. They had one pint every day and, once a week, eggs. He brought the milk to the kitchen. On a shelf were two bowls, two plates, two cups and a half-pint glass mug for beer. In the drawer were two forks, two knives, one dull and one sharp, two spoons, one small and one large, a battered soup ladle, a pair of rusty shears and a cleaver. On the worktop were a board and a bread knife. Two burned and bashed saucepans hung on hooks over the stove. The kettle, black and dented, stood precariously on the gas ring. Stuck in the oven was a greasy frying pan. They had everything they needed.

Mad Martin ate the same breakfast every day. He would put a careful measure of cereal into his bowl, pour on his allotment of milk, and take the bowl and spoon into the front room where he stood by the window and slurped away, staring out into Mop Street. He watched the same people going past the window, hurrying or walking slowly, and they wore the same coats or different coats and Mad Martin only vaguely recognized them and did not reflect on their comings and goings. By the time he had finished his cereal, it was time for school and his grandfather would be slowly making his way down the stairs, holding on to the walls and easing one large painful foot down after the other.

"What about teeth?" his grandfather always called out and Mad Martin would obediently run back to the kitchen, swish a cupped palmful of water in his mouth, spit and answer, "Yeh!"

"Zbògom," his grandfather would say which was his way of saying goodbye in the language of the faraway country he had come from. "Bye," and Mad Martin would be off to school. This is the way it was. Always the same sameness.

Of course the seasons changed, even cats knew that. A change of season meant a change of clothes, leaving off his pullover or putting it back on again or there came the time for wearing the coat that was too short in the sleeves and Mad Martin sometimes wondered if the sleeves wouldn't shrink up to his elbows before a new coat was forthcoming. He didn't really mind. Only it was hard to bend down to pick up fallen books and even harder to get arms in and out again. Unless it was very very cold, he left the coat at home.

Once a year there was Christmas when they had a celebration. Mad Martin would know Christmas was coming by the change in the window of the shop on the corner. All year long the window was full of stacked-up tins of peas, nothing much to take notice of. But one day in early December, Mad Martin would pass the shop as usual and in the corner of his eye something would twinkle and then he couldn't help noticing the disappearance of peas. Instead, there were stacked-up tins of Christmas puddings, and a space left in front for the Christmas scene. It was always the same: white cotton wool piled up to look like snow, little green trees stuck in the snow, and a lot of glittery dust sprinkled over the tins of Christmas puddings.

This was always the way of Christmas, when the peas went and the puddings came, and Christmas was also waking up and finding sweets in the sock he hung by the electric fire: jelly babies and a bar of chocolate and maybe pink-and-white coconut ice. And he would get a toy or a puzzle wrapped up in colored paper. His grandfather would have a pint of beer and get a packet of papers and some tobacco and he would roll up thin cigarettes which smelled bad when they were lit and puffed on, making smoke. The smell of this smoke would stay in the house for the whole of the school holiday. Mad Martin would know Christmas was over when the smell went and school came.

At Christmas and other school holidays, Mad Martin's diary changed slightly. It started out as usual, with getting up and eating breakfast but then it would be going out to the shops instead of to school. His grandfather would send him to buy matches and bread and packets of tea, glad that Mad Martin was home so he could save some wear and tear on what he called his "poor old dogs," meaning his feet. And the television would be blaring in the afternoon and

Mad Martin would push junk around or watch out the window or go two streets over where he could walk across the railway bridge and stare down at the passing trains.

Mad Martin had no particular preference about seasons, it was school mostly or holidays sometimes. But it was always on the holidays that he seemed to get a spell of the Bad Time. That's what he named it although he wasn't sure what it was exactly. A feeling of strangeness came over everything familiar. He would disappear into long blanks in his mind and not know the time was passing. Funny smells got into his nose and pains deep inside where his guts were and he would look at his cereal or his fish and not feel hungry, or he would look at the chairs in the front room and at his grandfather's poor old dogs in their ragged slippers and he would feel afraid of those things. He felt in danger of disappearing inside himself. If he closed his eyes, he might float up near the ceiling. Even worse, he might get the idea that he was on a big machine that kept turning and turning him around. Then he would wish his grandfather would talk to him, say things to make sounds, fill up the room with words to chase away the Bad Time. But his grandfather never said much of anything. He was quiet and silent, he didn't like to be bothered. He snoozed in his chair and Mad Martin watched him snoozing and felt afraid. He thought about how they were there in the room, two bodies with souls inside them. His grandfather was sleeping but who knew what the soul inside might be thinking? As for Mad Martin's own soul, it felt like an extra person had got in there uninvited. It felt like his body was one person and the thing inside was another.

After having a spell of the Bad Time, he walked gingerly and shaky. If the wind blew, he thought it might blow him over. He had to take small cautious steps and hold his arms close in to his sides. He stared at the ground to see where he was walking and bumped into people and things. Yet he felt a lot better when the Bad Time was over. He always wished it would never come again.

But even the Bad Time took its place in the sameness and that was the way it was: usual, same, always and forever.

Chapter 2

♨♫♫♫♫ One day, the sameness changed. It started out as usual. School was usual, which meant sitting quietly and unmoving for long hours, hearing the teacher's voice saying things up front, opening exercise books and writing until you got a crick in the fingers, closing books and sometimes gazing out the window at the gray sky. In the classroom, nobody said much to Mad Martin and he said nothing except to give an answer if the teacher asked him. He never got into trouble because he never did anything bad. If the teacher stepped out of the room for a minute and the boys started acting up, Mad Martin would scrunch low in his seat and stare at his desktop and shut his ears and let the boys run or shout around him. A long time ago they expected him to join in but he never would. First they thought he was just a drip but now they knew he was mad and potty and barmy and they avoided his desk as if they somehow sensed it might be dangerous to rouse a crazy person to action.

At dinnertime it was a different story. There were lots of boys in the dining room, boys from the whole school and not all of them thought Mad Martin was dangerously weird, only weird, and so they said nasty things to him and bumped and pushed him in the queue and tried to get him to spill his dinner. They could get away with this easily because it was a well-known fact that Mad Martin never grassed. If he spilled his dinner and a teacher told him to clean it up, Mad Martin did as he was told. He never mentioned that it was somebody else's fault. In fact, he never thought much about faults at all. The dinner was spilled and had to be cleaned up and that was all there was to it.

After dinner they were sent out into the school yard to stand around or play games for recess. Mad Martin had a special place near the fence, under the hanging branches of a large bush and if it was a good day, he could wait there until it was time to go back inside and not be bothered by anyone. He could stand under the branches and imagine he was out of his body and on his way to people's heaven, not forever squashed and dead but just a short trip to pass the time of waiting, and it was peaceful unless somebody came along and gave him a shove or a jab and brought him sharply back to bodily life.

On the way back to class, they would trip him up on the stairs and make him fall but he would rub his bruised knees surreptitiously under his desk and after a while the pain went away and by the time school was over he forgot all about it because even unpleasant things could fit into the pattern of sameness.

And so he came home on the usually usual day and opened the front door of the house and inside everything was unusual.

For one thing, there were two people sitting in the two chairs in the front room and neither one was his grandfather. In fact, they were ladies. For another thing, there was a smell in the house he had never smelled before. It crept up his nose and gave him a headache. The smell got in the way of his properly observing the two ladies and it was some time before he could take it all in. He blew his nose in his sleeve. He blinked to get the headache out of his eyes and he looked at them. One lady was young and one not so young. The not so young one was eating a bar of chocolate. The young one was smoking a cigarette. She had one of the kitchen plates in her lap and was using it for an ashtray. He stared at the plate, feeling very strange, and tried to think what his grandfather used when it was Christmas and he had his smelly rollups burning. He couldn't get it straight in his mind and felt confused. Maybe I'm in the wrong house, he thought hopefully, but the recognizable presence of the two chairs and table and television set convinced him he was not. He didn't know what he should do. He stood in the doorway blinking and sniffing and they looked at him.

"Martin Drivic?" one of them asked. The words scattered around in his head in a peculiar way. He nodded.

"Well come on then, come in," the not so young one said and heaved herself out of the chair and came over to him. He backed away.

"I won't bite," she said, laughing and tried to take his hand. He stuck both hands in his pockets.

"Just look at the state of him," she said, over her shoulder to the other one. He wondered what the state of him was and why she sounded worried about it. She broke off a big piece of her bar of chocolate and offered it. Mad Martin kept his hands in his pockets and looked at the floor. He felt thirsty and wanted a drink of water.

"Come and sit down," she said and pulled him against his will across the room. But she sat down in the chair again and he was left standing, wondering where he should sit.

"Don't worry," the other one said. She put the cigarette between her lips and sucked at it. Mad Martin watched, fascinated as the smoke came out of her nose.

"Now there's nothing to worry about," they said. "It's your grandfather," they said. Mad Martin suddenly thought of Shirley and felt afraid.

"I'm going in there," he said, using his polite school voice and, not waiting for their opinion, quickly ran to the kitchen. Immediately he knew the smell was coming from somewhere close by and he went into the dark cramped toilet and found its source. On the floor was a tall thin bottle of brownish liquid. It had a label saying Jeyes Disinfectant. Mad Martin picked the bottle up and read the label several times. He had never seen anything like it before. When he put it down the smell stayed on his fingers.

"Where are you?" called an anxious voice. "Where are you?" it demanded but then, seeing where he was, said, "Oh," and nothing more. He waited inside the smelly room, the door hooked, and thought if he stayed there long enough they would get tired of waiting and go away. He thought about people's heaven and his grandfather who was not in the house. He thought about his grandfather's squashed body somewhere without a soul and not counting. He thought he could not stay inside the toilet forever and he pulled the chain and came out.

The both of them were in the kitchen, taking up all the space and making him feel suffocated.

"I'd put the kettle on," the chocolate eater said, looking all around the kitchen and at the crusty stove. "But . . ." she said, all dismayed.

"Never mind," the other one said, taking charge all of a sudden. She made them go back to the front room where she sat Mad Martin down in one chair and stood herself in the center of the floor and delivered a speech. It was long, involved and complicated but Mad Martin was able to grasp a few facts. Mr. Drivic had fallen down and damaged his hip. This was to be expected in old age, Mad Martin was told and, although not serious in itself, was something to create problems. These problems had to do with him, Mad Martin. His welfare, whatever that might be. Therefore, he was to be looked after by the chocolate eater, Mrs. Crimp was her name, until such time as his grandfather was well again. He was to be in Mrs. Crimp's care with nothing to worry about.

"We'll just clean you up first," said Mrs. Crimp, "before I take you home."

"No," said Mad Martin. "I'm not going."

"Just for a short while," said Mrs. Crimp. "When your grandad is out of hospital, he'll be back to look after you again."

"No," said Mad Martin but Mrs. Crimp ignored this and made him come with her to the kitchen where, after a long search for a clean washcloth and towel, she proceeded to scrub his face. As he was being throttled and mauled with the wet washcloth, a conversation went on above his head, having to do with getting his things and finding his toothbrush which was nonexistent as Mad Martin could have told them had he been given half the chance.

When the washcloth moved away from his eyes and toward his ears, Mad Martin observed Mrs. Crimp. She was large but not so large as his grandfather. She had hair stuck on top of her head and fastened there with worm-shaped clips. The skin on the tops of her arms wobbled as she pushed the washcloth into the recesses of his ears. She smelled better than the toilet with its bottle of disinfectant. This was all he could take in at the time. He shut his eyes and let her push his chin back to get at his neck. All the while she muttered to herself and made tsking sounds with her mouth and for reasons unknown to Mad Martin sounded very disapproving. From a distance, it seemed with his eyes shut, he heard the other one saying, "Well now," and "Oh dear," and things were being moved around.

Then he was dried and pronounced shining and asked if he wanted to bring anything special along in the way of games or toys and told not to forget his school books. From upstairs, the younger voice complained, "But that is all there is! I can't find any more clothes or anything!"

Mad Martin said nothing. Silently he gathered up a few puzzles from his box under the table. He took his diary and his school books and it was all like he was in a fog until he noticed the plate with the squashed cigarette lying in it. Then he felt very funny, felt in danger of a Bad Time coming and couldn't do anything but stare at the plate. He felt a hand on his shoulder giving him a little shake and it woke him up. Mrs. Crimp stood next to him like a mountain, shaking her head way up on top as she made a parcel of his clothes. The other one wrote on a lot of papers in her lap. Mad Martin watched the pen moving on the papers and heard the scruff scruff sound it made as it formed the letters of words he could not read. Then the papers were put into a large purse and there was a feeling of hustle and bustle and the front door was thrown open, letting the air of the street come blowing in the room.

"Off we go," said Mrs. Crimp. Mad Martin stayed standing where he was.

"Come along, off we go," said Mrs. Crimp, and she gave

him a slight push and he went forward, looking at his feet, hardly aware that he was carrying his school books and diary and puzzles out the door. The puzzles rattled and slid.

"Wait a moment," said Mrs. Crimp and she and the other one went back into the kitchen and there was a thrashing around until they came out with a plastic carrier bag. Mad Martin knew the bag had holes in the bottom but he put his puzzles and diary in without a word and held on to the handles and allowed himself to be led out of his house by Mrs. Crimp and the other one with the large purse.

They said goodbye on the step. The purse went bouncing off down Mop Street. Mrs. Crimp led Mad Martin toward the bus stop. As he walked, pieces of puzzle fell out of the holes in the bag and skittered along the pavement. He watched them go over the side of the curb and into the road but he said nothing.

The ride on the bus was not long and perhaps they were going not very far away but for Mad Martin it was a confusing journey and he got off in a strange street and didn't know where he was. Mrs. Crimp, however, was full of confidence as she trotted along and Mad Martin's legs grew weary keeping up with her. At last they came to a house. It was not so very different from his own house and he felt relieved. It was joined to other houses on either side, it had three steps up to the front door and there were net curtains in the front window.

It will be the same, Mad Martin thought as he waited for Mrs. Crimp to find her key but as soon as the door was opened he saw that it would not be the same at all.

There were *things* everywhere. So many things that Mad Martin's eyes bulged. There were large chairs and small chairs and a big long double chair and pillows and tables and rugs and lamps and what looked like toys scattered all over the mantel above the electric fire: statues of dogs and birds and people in costumes and even cups and saucers of a kind Mad Martin had never seen before, all full of colors and pictures. More pictures on the walls and books on shelves and pots with green plants growing in them on the windowsill and a contraption in the corner which Mad Martin couldn't figure out. Seeing all of it so all of a sudden made Mad Martin shake.

As if that wasn't enough, he was rushed through the room of things into another that was even more upsetting. He could tell by the presence of sink and stove that he was in a kitchen but it was nothing like his kitchen at home. Here there were more chairs and a big table and a whole wall full of dishes and more pots and pans than anyone could ever use in a whole life. Not only that, there were strange machines full of buttons and dials. There was no bathtub. Mad Martin looked around a second time to make sure. Well, he thought, they have a lot but they don't have a bathtub, and he felt better.

"Now I'll just show you where everything is," Mrs. Crimp said, dropping Mad Martin's small parcel of clothes on top of one of the machines that had a big round window in it. "You'll feel more at home when you know where everything is," she said.

"The cloakroom's through here," she pointed out and he thought of cloaks wrapped around knights and damsels in distress like in the book at school, only when Mrs. Crimp opened the door he found himself staring at a toilet.

"There's another one upstairs, and the bath, and you can see for yourself, this is the kitchen," and Mrs. Crimp laughed gaily and dragged him on. Halfway on, she noticed he was still clutching the carrier bag of toys and she stopped and pried his fingers loose and made him put it down. Mad Martin's fingers felt empty and lonely with nothing familiar to hold on to.

They went upstairs. "This is Mark and John's room, and across there's Kate and Susan, we've put Nicholas in with them temporarily as he's only a baby," Mrs. Crimp exclaimed, flinging open doors. "And this is Charlie's room, you'll be staying in here with him." She paused for a breath and Mad Martin stared into Charlie's room where he would be staying in with him and his mouth opened wider and wider.

The rooms were full of beds, full of things dripping off the beds, and full of curtains and stuffed rabbits and bears and engines and cars, full of everything everywhere. Also carpets. Mad Martin found himself thinking of his cold bare feet on the cold bare floor of his own room and he wondered why he had never thought of it like that before.

"They're out, I sent them all to the park so you could have a little time to make yourself at home," Mrs. Crimp said, not unkindly, and she led him down the hall to another door which she did not fling open. "Mr. Crimp and I have this room," she told him. "Now you don't go playing in there, that's one of the rules. We don't have many rules but the ones we have, we keep to," and she sounded stern. Mad Martin looked up at her and nodded. He understood perfectly about rules. They had rules in school and he never broke them. Rules protected him and kept the boys from doing worse rotten things than they did. He thought that here, rules would be useful and possibly protect him from them who were all out. He had no intention of breaking rules. He nodded to Mrs. Crimp and she smiled. He noticed that she'd got very small shiny teeth.

"They'll all be coming in for supper and you'll get to know one another," Mrs. Crimp said, leading him back downstairs and his feet didn't clamor and thud because even the stairs had carpets on them. "You'll be meeting them very soon," she said and it opened up a big hole in Mad Martin's stomach.

In the kitchen, Mrs. Crimp handed Mad Martin a towel. "Wash your hands first," she directed, "and you can help me with the table." He washed his hands although they had been washed just previously on Mop Street. He spun the slippery, flowery soap in his fingers and thought all this washing would take the skin clean off his bones. Then he heard a great lot of noise, laughing and talking, from somewhere close behind him and he felt the terrible drafty hole in his stomach getting larger and he wished he wasn't there.

It was Them coming, the Charlies and Marks and Kates and babies, he knew. He kept washing his hands, over and over, not wanting to turn around. Mrs. Crimp's big pink wobbly arm suddenly reached over his shoulder and turned off the taps. "Now here they are," she said. "Come and say hello. Say hello everybody. This is Martin." She introduced them, every one, and Mad Martin lost count and was only glad of meeting the baby whose funny watery eyes didn't seem interested. The other ones were all looking at him fierce, like they might suddenly growl and want to eat him up.

"Hello Martin," they said soberly, like in a church. They had to make a queue at the sink for the hand washing, there were so many of them, and then they took their places at the table and Mrs. Crimp showed him where to sit and there was a horrible silence until everyone started laughing and talking again.

Mad Martin sat down and put his own scrubbed hands between his knees and watched. Overflowing plates of food passed around and under his nose. Plates of everything. Boiled eggs in a bowl. Pieces of toasted bread stuck in a thing with a handle. Pots of jam with spoons standing up in the middle and dribbles all down the side. Sausages, greasy and brown. A big lump of yellow butter. An enormous teapot steaming under a hat and a huge jug of milk. Everyone was grabbing everything but Mad Martin sat with his hands between his knees. He felt strange, not hungry, like the Bad Time might be coming. Yet his tongue was getting all salivary what with all the everythings being passed under his nose. Then Mrs. Crimp was setting all of it on a plate in front of him and tipping an egg into a blue-and-white cup so that it sat up, straight and still, waiting to be cracked open. Mad Martin marveled at the cup that could keep an egg standing so straight. "Come on then," said Mrs. Crimp. "Don't be shy." Mad Martin wasn't shy, just petrified.

"Is your grandad poorly?" asked the girl called Kate. She was little and low in her seat and her chin barely reached over the table's edge. Mad Martin looked at his egg and didn't answer. "His grandad's going to be fine," Mrs. Crimp answered for him.

"Why d'you have on that urggy shirt?" asked one of the boys. The boy called Charlie, older and wiser, punched him in the ribs to shut up. "I was only asking," the boy insisted, ate some toast and said, "It is urggy, anyway."

"Is he foreign?" asked Kate. "Why doesn't he speak?"

"Is he deaf?" they asked. "His egg's getting cold, can I have it?"

"Are you going to be interesting?" The same Kate kept

on wanting to know things. "We don't mind having them when they're interesting," she said. She gave Mad Martin a good long stare and then addressed the table. "He isn't going to be interesting."

"That's enough, Kate," said Mrs. Crimp. "More eating and less talk." Kate, looking miffed, bit her lip and cracked at her egg with great aplomb. Mad Martin could not help noticing how the warm syrupy yellow richness came out onto Kate's spoon. He thought about how it would be to taste that yellowy egg in his mouth. But he did nothing.

"Do you like football?" Charlie asked in a friendly way, as if to make up for Kate's remarks. "We have a target in the yard, to practice passing. If you like, you can have a go at it later." Charlie looked at Mad Martin expectantly. Mad Martin looked down at his egg.

"Well, do you like football or not?" asked one of the younger boys.

"Yeah, do you like it or not?" asked the other. One was Mark and one was John but Mad Martin couldn't remember which. They looked exactly the same except that one had sticking out teeth. Mad Martin looked at the teeth and back down at his plate.

"Perhaps," said Kate who had polished off her egg, "he doesn't care for football. Not everyone cares for football, you know. Not everyone's so daft as all of you are." Having given Mad Martin her support, she turned toward him and said earnestly, "I don't mind if you don't play football, Martin."

"He don't know nothing about it," said either Mark or John.

"Yeh, you can tell, he don't know a thing," said the other.

20

"Never mind them," said Kate. Her chin, delicately pointed, rested momentarily on her demolished egg and came away covered with yellow.

The boys laughed. One of them threw some toast. It missed Kate and hit Mad Martin in the nose.

"Manners!" admonished Mrs. Crimp. "Wipe your face, Kate." She gave a stern glance around the table and stopped short at Mad Martin. "Martin," she said, "please eat your food before it gets cold."

"He's skinny," one of the boys said.

"It's rude to say skinny," said Kate.

"What do you say then?"

"You say thin," said Kate primly.

"He's thin then."

"That's rude as well," said Kate.

"What's rude?" piped Susan who had all along been sitting quietly eating sausages.

"I know what's rude," said the Mark or John and giggled. They whispered to each other and Mad Martin felt terrible.

"Stop that," said Mrs. Crimp.

"Tell me what's rude," said Susan, and she fixed a stare at the sausage on Mad Martin's plate.

"You'd better eat your sausage," advised Kate in a motherly way. "Otherwise *she'll* want it," and she gave Susan a scathing glance.

"I won't either," said Susan who had already eaten four sausages. "I want a piece of jam."

"You can't have a piece of jam," said Kate and she smiled over at Mad Martin to see if he would share the joke. When he didn't respond she sighed. "I don't think he's going to be very interesting. Perhaps he's been starved."

"Oh good," said Susan.

"Tell us," the boys shouted. "Tell us how you've been starved!"

"Did they chain you up?" Susan wanted to know. "They always chain them up when they're starving them. They put them in a dungeon and feed them soup with mice floating in."

"Naw they don't," someone said and a hot argument began as to how to go about starving someone and the best way to do it.

Mad Martin thought about picking up a piece of the toasted bread. He thought about the yellowy egg and the brown sausage. He watched them all talking and eating things with spoons and forks and knives and spreading jam swiftly and neatly and wiping their hands on square white paper things and he thought they must all be very rich and related to the Queen and he got up from the table and ran away, ran to the stairs where he sat huddled and alone and his eyes felt like they were burning and itching, and his throat felt tight and choked.

"Oh my," Mrs. Crimp said. "Now look what you've done," and the children cried, "We haven't done anything," in unison and one of them called, "Come back, old Martin," but Mad Martin huddled deeper into the stair carpet and shut his ears and eyes.

He became aware that someone was standing near him and he opened an eye and looked. It was Kate, standing there twisting her braids around her fingers and observing him as if he were a specimen. "He's not crying," she reported, looking as serious and frightening as a doctor. "But he's not smiling either."

She knelt down and looked into his bleary eye. "If you

would only try," she whispered, "it would help. We'll get awfully weary of trying if you won't try just a little yourself."

Mad Martin's education had begun.

Chapter 3

ⱅⱅⱅⱅⱅⱅ   The first thing he had to learn about was smiling. This bothered everybody. "Smile," they all coaxed and wanted to know why he was so grumpy.

Well of course Mad Martin knew what a smile was, he wasn't that daft. He knew you smiled at something very funny, when someone acted in a pantomime, for instance, or did silly things, then you smiled. But then, Mad Martin had always found himself drifting off into a blankness at school plays and pantomimes and he couldn't remember getting a chance to smile at anything very funny very often. But the fact was, he knew what a smile was. Only here, at the Crimps, everyone seemed to smile all the time, for no reason. There wasn't anyone acting out a pantomime to make them smile, they just did it. It seemed like a smile was a permanent fixture on the face of every Crimp.

Mad Martin stood secretly in the cloakroom and looked into the mirror and tried a smile. He stretched his lips deep into his cheeks on either side and saw his teeth appear, brown and motley, and somehow it didn't look like what they called smiling.

When something funny happens, he thought, then I'll smile.

The other thing was talking. "Talk," they encouraged. "Tell us things." Mad Martin could not fathom what it was he should be telling them. They waited but Mad Martin said nothing.

They, on the other hand, talked all the time. He wondered where they got so much talking from, it just poured out of their mouths like water from a tap. He thought about his own house where it was mostly quiet and silent. His grandfather snoozing in front of the television and himself pushing his junk around on the floor. He and his grandfather only talked when they had to say something about something. Like "Shut the window," or "Go to bed," or "Where's my slipper?" That was when you did talking. In school, the teacher talked endlessly but that was to teach lessons. In school also, the boys talked at dinnertime to say things about the boiled cabbage and how it smelled or complain about the pudding or sometimes to say remarks about women's "things" and tell what was called filthy jokes but Mad Martin never said any. But all that kind of talking was nothing like Crimp talking which was just talking talking talking all the time, like saying your dreams out loud.

"Come on, tell us," they kept on. "Tell us."

"What?" Mad Martin was forced to ask.

"Everything," they said. "Like about your grandad, did they send an ambulance to take him to hospital? Was there any blood? Did you cry?"

"I don't know," said Mad Martin.

They didn't believe him. "Why not? Why don't you know? Why won't you tell us?"

"I don't know," Mad Martin said and the tight feeling came back in his throat and the hole in his stomach started blowing gales.

"Leave him alone," said Charlie.

"He's all sad," said Kate. "Anyone can see that."

But Mad Martin didn't feel sad. He just felt like he'd like to be a ghost, like he'd like to be invisible so he could go somewhere quiet and not be asked to talk or smile ever again.

At last, when it was time to turn the television on and everyone sat down to watch, Mad Martin had a chance to be left alone. "You can sit next to me," Kate had offered but Mad Martin found a place away from them, in the corner, and he sat down and looked toward the television screen but he didn't see it and he didn't hear it. Instead he was thinking about who they all were. Kate and Susan might be sisters and Mark and John were brothers and there was Charlie, but Mad Martin wasn't sure if they were all Crimps or just some Crimps and others like him, being looked after until maybe their grandfathers who were in hospital could come home and take them back again. He wondered if the ones who weren't Crimps were wishing they could be left alone. He thought about this for a while and then the nice comforting blankness came over him and he just sat and thought nothing. And then it was ruined by a big commotion. Someone was coming in the door and everyone was saying "Dad" and "Daddy" and Mad Martin suddenly knew that all the Charlies and Kates and babies belonged to Mr. and Mrs. Crimp, were their children, and he was the only non-Crimp in the lot.

All of them jumped on Mr. Crimp and sat on him and pulled and yanked and all the while Mr. Crimp was smiling and talking until he had had enough and said, "Get off!" Mad Martin stood in the corner, furtively watching and recalling that he had never jumped on or yanked at his grandfather. He felt odd and creepy even at the thought of it.

He was in awe of Mr. Crimp who was very tall and full of hair. Mr. Crimp put out a hand and said, "How do you do, Martin," and Mad Martin stared at the hand until finally Mr. Crimp took it back again.

"He's sad," Kate told her father confidentially. "His grandad's poorly and he might have been starved."

"Who? His grandfather?" asked Mr. Crimp, looking startled.

"That's enough, Kate," said Mrs. Crimp and she took Mr. Crimp's overcoat and hung it up and told them it was time to go upstairs.

Upstairs in the bedroom, he and Charlie looked at each other and Charlie shuffled his feet around on the rug. "We don't have to go to sleep," Charlie said. "This is just the quiet time. But we should get undressed. Have you got your pajamas?"

Mad Martin looked around as if expecting to see his possessions somewhere in the room. "I don't know," he said. He did have some pajamas somewhere but he wasn't sure if Mrs. Crimp and the other lady had taken them from his room. Now that he came to think of it, he couldn't recall when he had seen those pajamas last. Mostly he didn't wear them. He slept in his underwear and, if it was cold, he put on his pullover and kept his socks on. Anyway, he was never cold because on his bed he had a kush, this being what his grandfather called the huge warm feather-filled quilt. It could get sweating hot in there and he would have to kick it off but by morning he would be freezing and had to wake up and pull it back on again. Mad Martin looked at the beds in Charlie's room and saw a poor replica of his kush on each one. This gave him a burst of confidence and he said, "I don't wear pajamas."

"Never mind, you can borrow some of mine," said Charlie. Mad Martin did not protest as he was handed the pajamas. They were blue-and-yellow and very soft.

Charlie was busy stripping off his clothes. Mad Martin turned away and slowly unbuttoned himself. He felt peculiar getting undressed with someone else in the room. He wondered if he should leave his underwear on or take it off when he wore the pajamas. Thinking of the puny kush, he decided to leave it on.

"That vest of yours sort of hums, don't it?" he heard Charlie say. He turned but Charlie wasn't looking at him, he was tying his pajama strings. "You can put it in the dirty clothes basket over there," he told Mad Martin and pointed.

Mad Martin looked down at his vest. It was his usual vest, as always, the one he'd had on for two weeks. But he knew what hum meant all right. It meant dirty rancid reeking like the flies might buzz around. He understood now about the urggy shirt business at supper. Not only was his shirt urggy but Charlie thought his underwear was even urggier. He went over to the dirty clothes basket and lifted the lid. Inside, it looked like all clean clothes, not dirty ones. He pulled off his undershirt and threw it in and the contrast was amazing. His vest looked like a lump of old mud. He quickly put the lid back down. He got Charlie's pajamas on and buttoned just in time because Mrs. Crimp walked into the bedroom. "Oh," she said.

"I lent him some pajamas," Charlie told her.

"That's very nice of you, dear," said Mrs. Crimp. "But wouldn't it be nicer if Martin had a bath first?"

The burning and tightness came back to Mad Martin's throat. His face felt all hot. Charlie and his mother were talking about him as if he wasn't there, not asking him if he wanted any bath, just deciding it for him. He wondered who was going to carry all the pots of hot water up all the stairs to fill the bathtub. I'm not doing it, Mad Martin thought. It's not my idea.

But Mad Martin found himself sitting in a bath which had taps as well as a drain and didn't need to be filled up with pots of boiling water from the stove. And whereas his previous baths had been lowly affairs, the water not much above his knees, this bath was huge and overflowing and Mad Martin wondered if he might not drown.

He sat in the bath and felt a feeling of some kind of badness coming over him. He felt, what was the word, ashamed. Ashamed for all his urgginess.

Slowly, with the help of all the drowning hot water and lots of soap, bright pink lobster skin emerged where before there had only been a dull gray smear. When he pulled the plug and all the water had gone down the drain, a nasty dark ring was left around the tub like a leftover reminder.

I don't care anyway, thought Mad Martin. It has nothing to do with me.

Later on, he learned about kissing. He wasn't prepared for it and was taken unawares. Mrs. Crimp made the rounds of all the bedrooms, saying goodnight. She came into Charlie's room and bent herself double and smacked a wet juicy kiss down on Mad Martin's forehead. He was appalled. He wasn't even sure what had transpired. Then he was being tucked up, the bed clothes all stuck in underneath around him until he couldn't move his hands or feet.

Mrs. Crimp plumped up the meager kush. "Goodnight," she said. "Pleasant dreams."

"G'night," Charlie said to her but Mad Martin said nothing.

"Tomorrow I'll show you my camp," confided Charlie after the door was shut on them. Mad Martin didn't answer.

"It's a secret place I have," Charlie said. "I have booby traps to keep out yobs." Mad Martin was silent.

"I'll let you see it, though. What's the matter, are you feeling knackered or something?"

With great effort, Mad Martin forced himself to reply, "Yeh," hoping to close the conversation.

"Well, goodnight for now," said Charlie. Then it was all quiet.

Mad Martin lay trapped in the bed and wished he was back at home. He thought of the ways he could have escaped from the two ladies in the front room, how he could have run to the railway bridge and stayed till dark and they would have given up waiting and gone away. He thought about being home in his bed, home all alone in the house and he didn't think he would mind. He could have gone on doing all the things he had always done, taking in the milk and eating his cereal and getting fish and chips for supper. He could look after himself without much trouble. His grandfather had only been in the background, a presence, not like Mrs. Crimp with her hand washing and kissing. He and his grandfather had done okay without worrying about baths and humming vests.

He thought that here was a house full of everything and too many people and he would do much better without it all.

They could have left him a note, and a small amount of

money, that's all that was needed. It would have been simpler. Yes, Mad Martin thought, pleasant dreams, he remembered. He wondered if dreams were like the soul taking a trip while the body stayed behind. He thought it must be so. Sleeping and dreams were only practice for when you finally had to leave your body forever.

Chapter 4

🔗🔗🔗🔗🔗 Nobody tied their shoes with strings. Everybody had a toothbrush. Soon Mad Martin would have one too, promised to be brought home that evening by Mr. Crimp.

Mad Martin sat at the breakfast table and felt different. He did not put his hands between his knees. Instead he took some of everything that was passed to him and ate it all because he was hungry and he paid no attention to anybody. He didn't answer when spoken to and he didn't use his square paper napkin. He felt like a kettle heating up on the gas ring and just let them mention urggy shirts and then would he boil! He had resentments, only he didn't know that's what you called them.

"What's the matter with him, do you think?" asked Susan but Mrs. Crimp shushed her. In a way, Mad Martin was sorry she had been shushed because he would have liked to say what was the matter with him, and would have liked to say what was the matter with them as well but on the other hand it was easier and better not to say anything. Let them think what they thought and so what. He would just wait out the days, eating and sleeping, until it was time to go home again.

Mrs. Crimp wanted to know if he knew how to get back after school. She drew a map on one of the paper napkins and told him the number of the bus ten times. "I'll ring up and find out how your grandad's getting along," she told him, "and I'll tell you the news when you get home."

"Which home?" Mad Martin asked.

"Why, here, of course," Mrs. Crimp said, amazed at the question.

"This is Crimps," said Mad Martin. "Not home."

"All right then, Crimps," said Mrs. Crimp and she laughed and it was Mad Martin's turn to be amazed because he didn't consider it funny, it was very serious. "We'll do our best," she added, "to make this your home away from home until your grandad is better." Then she hustled and bustled everybody, reminding them not to forget their books and hats and what all. Mad Martin had everything ready. He stood near the door, feeling out of sorts because it wasn't at all like his typical morning with his grandfather wheezing down the stairs and calling out about teeth and saying Zbògom. Crimps wouldn't know what Zbògom meant so he wasn't going to say it to them.

Mr. Crimp came along to show Mad Martin how to get to his school, because Charlie and the others went to theirs a different way. Once out of sight of the Crimp house and once rid of Mr. Crimp, Mad Martin began to feel more usual. He pretended he had never heard of Crimps. He pretended he was going to school from his own house and that everything was usual.

All day he pretended it was the same as always. He sat at his desk and listened to the teacher and diligently wrote his lessons. He stopped up his ears at dinnertime and afterward went and waited under the bush and it was a good peaceful time because nobody came near him. It was quite easy to forget all about Crimps and he soon did.

But when the day was over and it was time to go home, he found himself walking in the wrong direction. Right direction for home but wrong for Crimps. He stopped and considered. There was no reason why he shouldn't go home after all. He knew where there was a key hidden near the front steps, put there by his grandfather in fact, for just such an emergency as a damaged hip. They had hidden it together a long time ago but it was probably still in the same place. Mr. Drivic was always home in the afternoon, but once, years ago, he had trouble with a bad eye and had to make weekly trips south of the river to a special hospital. One afternoon the underground train got stuck and Mr. Drivic was late. Mad Martin couldn't get in the door and he waited on the doorstep, hunched and cold and full of not knowing what to do because such a thing had never happened before. When he caught sight of his grandfather's lumbersome figure making its way slowly down Mop Street, he was filled with a kind of wild elation, all of a sudden realizing that he had been worrying that he would never see his grandfather again. He jumped off the step and went running to meet him.

"Grandpa, Grandpa," Mad Martin had cried, streaking down the street, full of happiness. But his grandfather had put out a defensive arm, waving his stick with the other to keep Mad Martin from knocking him over.

"Yes, yes, it's the grandpa," he said and seemed annoyed and irritable. Mad Martin felt deflated. He walked soberly back to the house at his grandfather's side and said nothing about his worries or his joy. His grandfather sat down in the chair in the front room and stayed there a long time catching his breath. "No more, no more," he said, no more would he go on such long journeys but later he had taken Mad Martin outside in the dark and they had hidden the key in the loose stones near the ground. If ever Mad Martin came home and found the door locked, he could get the key and let himself in and close the door and be safe and under no circumstances was he to trouble the neighbors. "Keep to yourself," his grandfather warned him. "Don't go pestering neighbors," and he looked around suspiciously and hurried Mad Martin back inside.

Mad Martin felt prodded by a question and he asked it. "But what if you don't come home for a very long time, will it be all right to pester the neighbors then?" His grandfather shook his head and made the na-na sound which meant he was not pleased. Have nothing to do with neighbors, his grandfather said again, never speak to neighbors who are nosy and want to know your business. Keep your business to yourself. And so they kept their business between themselves inside the house and never let anybody else come in. His grandfather wanted nothing to do with nobody.

Remembering this, Mad Martin was on the lookout for nosy neighbors as he dug out the key. It was rusty but when he stuck it into the lock it turned and the door opened. He walked in.

The funny smell was still there but it was fading. All the other smells were familiar and the same. It was home. He shut the door and stood in the room and listened and the house was quiet and still, listening back at him.

The hush made him take off his shoes and creep noiselessly into the kitchen where he turned the taps to see if they were working which they were and he took a cup and had a drink of water which tasted foul. He spat it out and the sound of running water suddenly seemed too loud and boisterous. He quickly turned it off.

He wanted to get on with doing what he usually did but

somehow he was standing in the kitchen not moving. Drip drip drip went the tap and he tried to make it tighter. From somewhere above there was a creak and then a crackling sound. He thought of his grandfather being up in his room and how his slippers sounded as they scuffled the bare floor. But his grandfather wasn't up there now, nobody was. Yet the more he listened, the more sounds there were all around him.

"No one is here," he told himself, "only me."

I'm hungry, he thought. I'll have tea now. The Crimps would be having their supper and he would be having his. He knew all about it. He didn't need all the everythings Crimps had.

He filled the kettle and put it on the gas. The tea caddy had only a bit of tea in the bottom but enough for him. There was the end of a loaf and it was very hard and had some green spots on it. He scraped them off. He could soak it in the tea and it would get soft enough to eat. He looked around for the pint of milk which was kept on the windowsill because they had no freezing cold refrigerator like Crimps. It was a shock to realize no pint of milk was there. Nobody took in the milk! and he ran to the door. None there either. Somebody's nicked it, he thought. Never mind, I'll have tea without.

He brought his cup and his hard heel of bread into the front room and sat in the chair. He looked all around the room and thought how much nicer it was not to be full of stuff like at Crimps. Yes it is better like this, he thought. Yes it is, he thought, less sure.

He sat and drank and gnawed and the late afternoon shadows came and played on the walls. He was alone in the house but in a way it was exactly like usual when his grandfather sat in the other chair snoozing, saying nothing. His grandfather. Not at all like Mr. Crimp who was trampled on when he came in the door. No trampling allowed on grandfather who would wave you off with his stick. None of all that noise like at Crimps what with all the smiling and talking. Reminded of Crimp smiles, Mad Martin contemplated. His grandfather did not smile very much. Perhaps he was grouchy? Or sad? What could he be sad about? To find out, he would have to ask and his grandfather didn't like pesty questions. Crimps asked questions all the time and they got answers out of you whether you liked it or not. Crimps were always running around doing things. His grandfather sat in the chair.

And yet, he thought, once, there was his grandfather standing in the room doing something. Dancing. Dancing funny, thudding his feet and slapping his trouser legs. Slap slap, bang went a foot, and slap and bang another foot, and then heels making loud noises to go with a song that his grandfather was singing.

But no, that couldn't be his grandfather. It must be a dream. A dream mixed up with life like sometimes happens.

The shadows flicked across the walls and Mad Martin thought of dreams. Dreams like when there were more people in the house, more people so that it was like a Crimp feeling in the house. He could remember a lady standing near the window with a cloth in her hand. A man carrying a bucket of water. The water spilling on the floor and Mad Martin making wet squishy stamping sounds with his bare feet in the puddle. Somebody laughing and then the feeling of flying through the air as he got picked up out of the puddle, feet dripping. The man and woman bending over him so that their heads touched and made a bridge. That would be his parents. A mother and father were once in the house, like at Crimps.

No, I don't remember that, Mad Martin thought. I don't know anything about that.

Shadows crawled across the walls and scuffles and creaks prowled around upstairs. No one is here, only me. But what if his grandfather's soul came back to find its slippers? That was stupid, his grandfather was not squashed, only in hospital, with his soul still inside his body. But the creaks were crawling and the back of Mad Martin's neck crawled too. He thought he better not turn around. He felt sure he would see something horrible, a big and ugly thing with its tongue hanging out. Looking at him. The big and ugly thing would slosh across the floor and it would go ahummm, eeerummmm, gaasaaaaa, and the huge mouth would be opening and closing and the tongue slobbering in and out. Then a fat hand would grab him, tear off his arms, gobble him. Getting gobbled, all full of spit, sliding down the throat of the monster and into its stomach. The stomach would be all curly and slimy like the tripe his grandfather cooked in a pot and stirred with a fork.

He looked with the corner of his eye and then he turned and the horrible thing wasn't there, only the empty oblong of black space where the stairs went up. He put down his cup and went to the stairs and looked into the dark. Would he go up there when it was time to sleep? What if the thing was up there, sleeping in his grandfather's bed? It would wake up and look at him from under the covers and it would make the sound, gaaaaa, aaaahhh, and it would plop onto the floor and squish. The mouth would start opening and closing and . . .

Outside in the street was a shout and the sound of a

motor. It brought Mad Martin back to himself. Fears receded momentarily. And then suddenly the dark room closed around him and he wanted to get out.

He pulled on his shoes and had trouble with the knots and as he bent down to fix them he felt frightened and wanted to crawl under one of the chairs and hide. Then he was up and out, laces dragging undone. He almost forgot to put the key back in its place. He hurried toward the bus stop. On the bus, sitting among other people, the idea of a monster lurking in the house seemed far away and stupid. Not even nearly real. The closer the bus brought him to Crimps, the more depressing was the prospect of facing their numbers. For a fleeting mad moment Mad Martin considered retracing his steps and confronting the shadows of his house again. And then he was off the bus and nearing Crimps. And then he was at the door. And then the door was opened and the Crimps began to sing. His ears were overcome by the noise of it.

Questions, questions, why was he so late?

"I knew it," cried Mrs. Crimp. "I knew you'd lose your way!"

He let her think that was the reason.

Chapter 5

There was this thing called hate. He'd heard about it. He decided he hated them. He locked himself in the cloakroom and considered this. He had never hated before. Perhaps it was only an illness coming on, this feeling, like a burning inside. He wanted to be sure.

Lying in the tucked-up bed, trapped by sheets but far less weighed down than when he was covered by his own kush, he asked Charlie, "Do you know anything about hate?"

"Uh?" said Charlie from the other bed. "What?"

"I've heard of people having this thing of hating. I wondered if you knew about it."

"Of course I know about it," Charlie said. "I mean, who doesn't?"

Maybe me, thought Mad Martin but he said, "Well do you have any?"

"Any what?"

"Any of this hate thing? Do you hate? Do you hate something?"

"Sure."

"What's it feel like?"

"I hate math and I hate stinking liver and I hate exams and I hate it when Mark busts up my camp and I hate

Nicholas when he cries all night except he doesn't do that much anymore and I hate lots of things, do you want me to keep on saying what?"

Mad Martin was overwhelmed. "You hate all that?" he asked.

"I told you, I hate more than that. Let's see, raisins, cutting my toenails, pigeons doing a mess on my camp roof, and other things, I just can't think of it all right now."

"But what's it feel like?"

There was a pause and the sound of turning over. "It feels like you don't like it."

"No," Mad Martin said. "Inside it must feel like something. Not in your head, not thinking it. Other places where you don't think. Places where you feel."

Charlie considered this. "I don't know. It's different for different things. An exam makes me worried like."

"No not that. Worried is still thinking. What's it feel like inside where it's all blood and guts?"

"Eeech," said Charlie. "Shut up."

Mad Martin felt like going over to Charlie's bed and shaking him to make him tell. "I want to know, I do," he said.

"Oh all right, I'll think." Charlie sounded exasperated. "I have to think it first. Well. An exam makes me sick, makes me feel like I don't want breakfast. I get all jitter jabbers inside my guts if you want to know. I feel ill."

This confirmed Mad Martin's thoughts. Feeling sick, like an illness coming on. Yes, that was it. Hate.

But something was still bothering him. "Charlie?" he asked the other bed. "Charlie. It's okay to hate, is it? It's not like a real disease?"

"Everybody does it all the time," Charlie replied. "What's up with you anyway?"

"Nothing," Mad Martin said.

So he hated them. It didn't interfere with things, he didn't need the doctor. The hate stayed inside like a big round ball, lodged in his stomach or nearaways. It could travel upward into his chest or throat. It could possibly come out of his mouth if he wasn't careful and that would mean telling them and he didn't want to, not right now. So he swallowed it down when it got near his mouth. He wanted his hate to be private because as long as it was private, the Crimps couldn't take it away.

Not that they took much away. Mostly they gave him things. They gave shirts and socks and a toothbrush. The socks were new but the shirts weren't. Mrs. Crimp washed and ironed them and tried to make them look new but they were old from somebody else, probably Charlie, and when Mad Martin had to put one on he felt like he was inside Charlie and in danger of becoming a Crimp. He made sure his real things were still there. He wanted to have his things, it was important.

The blue-and-yellow pajamas were all right. He didn't mind about them. The first morning he had taken them off and handed them back to Charlie but Charlie said, "They can be your ones for now," so he kept them. The socks had an advantage so he didn't mind about the socks too much either. They stayed up, that was the thing.

"These socks are full of holes," Mrs. Crimp said when she looked at Mad Martin's own private dirty ones. She poked her fingers around inside and they appeared out the toes and heels. She wagged them. "I don't know," she said, "perhaps," she said, eyeing the dustbin.

"I want them," Mad Martin burst out, making Mrs. Crimp jump.

"All right. I'll try to darn them," Mrs. sighed. That's what he called her now, in his mind: Mrs. "But I don't guarantee the results," Mrs. warned him.

Mad Martin needed his socks, holes or not. They were him and he was them. It was necessary.

Whenever the hate was in danger of cooling off, he rekindled it by finding grumpy things to grump about. Mostly the danger came at mealtimes. Then his stomach would betray him. It wanted the everythings now, it was used to them. The lump of hate would get pushed out of the way to make room for food. Then Mad Martin would make himself stop chewing and think hate for a few minutes. Hate hate hate, he would think as Mrs.'s fat pink arms reached across the table to set down another big bowl of steaming food. Look at them, look at them, he ordered himself, hate hate hate.

He had never looked at people closely before. But now, seeing as how he was face-to-face with Crimps almost every minute, he found himself looking very closely. There were Mark and John, alike as twins except for Mark's sticking out teeth. They had white light hair neatly trimmed around the ears and their elbows were sharp and jabbing all the time into one another as they argued. They were always putting things in their mouths, whatever came to hand, pencils, stones, chocolates if they could get some away from Mrs. who always had some in her pockets or her purse and never wanted to part with any of it.

There was Susan. She was unimportant. She took up in

43

other people's talk and kept on harping on a subject long after everyone else was finished. She wasn't much bother to Mad Martin except that she was like an echo of Kate.

Kate was properly the biggest hate. She asked too many questions. She gave too many opinions. She was thin and pointy and overly serious. She squinted up her eyes and stuck her nose in the air like she knew everything in the whole world. She could act like Mrs. exactly. Mrs. would shush her but Kate kept on. Her hair hung down all around her back and shoulders, straw colored. She wore elastic headbands which kept slipping off where she let them stay, limp around her neck. If she was concentrating hard and seriously, she would pull the band up around her mouth and chew on it.

There was Charlie. He was thin and all angles too, like all the Crimp children, so unlike their round mother who jiggled when she walked. Charlie's hair was brown and not cropped so close around his ears and he sometimes wore glasses. Sometimes, because he was always taking them off and losing them or putting them in his pocket and sitting on them so that the frames snapped. "Unbreakable lenses," Mrs. would despair. "But you find a way just the same!" She said Charlie would have to get a stick and tap his way to school like a blind man for all she cared, she was not going to be bothered anymore. Charlie said it didn't matter, he could hold a lens up to his eye if he wanted to read the number of the bus. "I don't like them," he confided to Mad Martin when they were alone, confidentially tucked up in their beds. "They bugger up and down your nose, they do." It was difficult hating Charlie but Mad Martin forced himself.

Nicholas the baby, Mad Martin left out of his hate, having no immediate gripes against it. And Mr. Crimp. Tall and overpowering that he was, Mr. Crimp was much too awesome a figure to hate. But some hate could be stuck on Mrs.—fat pink arms, for instance.

"I hate their hair," he told himself. It's all ratted up with bugs, he decided. And he would watch the nearest head closely to see if he could catch a bug crawling around. Bugs were bad, he knew from school. You had to get a special comb and find the nits. In the house on Mop Street they had no special comb but Mad Martin, fresh from a hygiene lecture, had come home and asked his grandfather to look for nits. His grandfather made the na-na sound and told him there were no bugs to worry about. But Crimps had bugs, he knew. Bugs would serve them right for all their washing and thinking he was urggy.

"That's rude," Kate would say if she noticed him staring at heads. She was always advising how to behave and acting like a nosy neighbor. "I think you must be sad," she told him. "Why don't you tell me what you're thinking?" she would say when she managed to catch him somewhere, on the stairs or in a corner. She lurked. Waiting to pounce. "I won't tell *them*," she promised. "We can have a secret."

"If it's a secret, only one person can have it," Mad Martin told her and was surprised and pleased when it shut her up. She went away. For a while.

Hate hate hate was burning away inside him. But hate was a confusing thing. Like the night the baby Nicholas did cry, all night long, and the next morning Mad Martin found Charlie playing with him in the kitchen. There was Charlie, making faces, and the baby laughing, still not tired. Mrs. was tired. She said, "Just watch him a moment," and went out of the kitchen. Mad Martin asked, "Why? You said you

45

hated him when he cried at night. Why aren't you hating him then? You're playing with him all happy like, and you're smiling. Tell me, do you smile when you have the hate?"

"Cooo," Charlie said, shaking his head. "I didn't mean it *that* way. Don't you know the difference between hating and really hating?"

And so it was a revelation to Mad Martin that there was hating and really hating. He reflected sadly that he did not know the difference. Yet.

He stopped looking for bugs. That was probably not really hating. Really hating was bigger and better. Bugs was nothing. Bugs was insignificant. He decided that anyway Crimps didn't have any bugs.

He reviewed all the things Charlie had told him he hated and Mad Martin came to the conclusion they were all unworthy of really hating. They were make-believe hates and if he looked inside himself, he discovered he had some of his own. Yes, he hated that cabbage smell the way the other boys did. And the soggy school puds. These were plain ordinary everyday hates, he just hadn't known what to call them before. Everybody had these. They helped you to know what didn't agree with yourself.

But *really* hating, what could that be? He wanted to be really hating the Crimps. Hate them for the bad things they did to him. Like calling him urggy and telling him his vest hummed and being made to have baths. The first two were good reasons for really hating but actually he liked the baths. He had never liked baths before he came to Crimps. But here it was baths hot and drowning and submerged up to the nose, being in an ocean alone, adrift and nobody else in the world. Still, it wasn't nice how they insisted. It made him feel he was different from all of them. It made him feel that Mrs. was thinking his grandfather was bad for not insisting on baths. Every time Mrs. told him to wash his hands or change his shirt or learn some proper table manners it was like she was saying that everything he and his grandfather had done on Mop Street was wrong. And if she was saying his whole former life was no good, well then he should hate her for that. Because who said she was right anyway?

But he didn't know if he was any closer to the answer of what really hating could be.

And while Mad Martin was wrestling with the problem of hate, he encountered a new kind of thing to feel. Not that he felt it. But he was told he must be feeling it. Love.

"You must love your grandad very much," Mrs. said, darning socks. "I'm sure you miss him." Mrs. had a special voice for when she said these things. All sort of churchlike. He was interested in the part about love.

Dragged into the yard by Charlie to practice kicks at the target, Mad Martin pondered the business of loving his grandfather very much. His mind was not on kicking. "Come on," Charlie said. "Come on, your go." Listlessly, Mad Martin stuck his foot out. Maybe he really hated football, he thought as he kicked the ball into the bushes, nowhere near the target.

"Bad luck," said Charlie. Mad Martin stared into the bushes but he wasn't thinking about the ball. He let Charlie fetch it. "You're not thinking," Charlie said patiently. But that was wrong. Mad Martin was thinking very hard.

Love was sometimes on the television when they kissed. They said, "I love you," to each other. It was not the kind of kissing Mrs. did, however. Goodnight kissing was not like television love kissing. Or perhaps love was like when his grandfather said, "I love a pint, aaaah!" making a kissing sound with his mouth and throwing up his hand, fingertips all kissed and stuck together. He did that at Christmas when he had beer in the glass mug. Or maybe it was like in school, loving honorable things that made people do brave acts.

"I was wondering," Mad Martin said. "I was thinking about this thing of loving. Do you know anything about it?"

Charlie was aiming for a kick and he missed. "Uh?" he said. "What?"

"Loving. I was wondering about it."

Charlie looked at him warily. "What about it?"

"Tell me a few things."

"What, about love?"

"Yes," Mad Martin said. "Please," he said, because all Crimps had to use that word if they wanted to get anything at all.

"It depends," said Charlie vaguely as he aimed for a kick again. "What exactly kind of love did you have in mind?"

"I don't know. Are there lots of kinds?"

Charlie made a choked up sound, suspiciously like a laugh. "Are you serious or what?"

"Of course," said Mad Martin feeling a little annoyed. But to show good faith he kicked the ball and almost hit the target.

"Not bad," said Charlie. Mad Martin waited. Charlie dug his heel into the scrabby grass of the yard. "I don't know why you want to know but well, there's all kinds. There's this love you're supposed to have for your parents, you know, that bit." Charlie dispensed with that bit by shrugging his shoulders. "Or you love where you go for a holiday. You like it so much you think you love it." Mad Martin could tell Charlie did not think much of this kind of love either. "Those are ordinary," he said, still digging his heel, "they're nothing special."

"What's the special one?" Mad Martin asked eagerly.

Charlie looked doubtful, as if he wasn't sure Mad Martin was worthy of knowing. Also he seemed embarrassed.

"Well," he muttered, "it's when you love your dog. Or your car."

Mad Martin was disappointed. "But how does it feel?" he wanted to know.

Charlie, remembering past quests for blood and guts, tried to drop the subject. Mad Martin would not let him.

"Come on, let's play," said Charlie.

"Not until you tell me. I must know," Mad Martin pleaded.

"You aren't half weird," Charlie told him and got ready to kick the ball again.

Mad Martin thought of the television kisses. "What about," he said, "when they show people kissing? A man and a lady, kissing each other. They say 'I love you' and other stuff. When they talk about the love they look like they're worried, or maybe they have a pain. They screw up their faces . . . like this," and Mad Martin gave a fair imitation of what he had seen on the television screen.

"Oh that," Charlie said. "That's sex."

"Sex." Mad Martin said the word.

"Yeah, sex. You know about that, don't you?" Charlie gave him such a penetrating look that Mad Martin found himself blurting, "Sure." But as Charlie seemed to think the discussion was ended, he had to add, "But if you tell me what you know about it, then I'll surely be sure."

Charlie whistled through his teeth. "Wheeeeew, you want me to tell you about sex?"

"Yes please," said Mad Martin.

"I bet you don't know anything."

Mad Martin felt uncomfortable. It was reminiscent of the way they said his shirt was urggy or to take a bath. Like they knew everything and he knew nothing. "I bet you don't either," he said and it was the right thing to say because it made Charlie talk.

"Well you know about having babies? That's sex, only you're not supposed to mention it to adults. They like you to think you get babies from under a bush or something and they get worried when you ask for details. When they finally admit that babies come out of stomachs, they won't tell you how. They tell you 'down there' but they won't say exactly where." Charlie paused, checked to see that no adults were listening and beckoned Mad Martin closer. "Now I can tell you the exact details. It's like this, see. . . ."

But Mad Martin wasn't interested in all that. "Babies," he said, feeling disappointed once again, "babies . . . is that the love?"

"It can happen," Charlie said, annoyed at being interrupted, "if you muck about with sex."

"Then is sex the special love, too, like loving your dog or your car?"

Charlie rolled his eyes around. "Don't be so daft. Sex is different altogether." He executed a kick and made a perfect target.

Mad Martin wasn't even looking, he was still pondering. "But what does this sex love feel like?"

"It feels all right, I expect, or they wouldn't be bothered doing it."

"Doing what?"

"What do you think? Doing sex!" and Charlie checked around over his shoulders again and then made a gesture with his fingers which Mad Martin recognized as the thing boys did at school which they were not supposed to. "See look, this is the man and this is the woman and this is the way it operates," Charlie said, sounding like a doctor and Mad Martin found it interesting but it still had nothing to do with what he wanted to find out about love.

"Did you ever do it?" he asked.

Charlie looked affronted. "You don't get to do it until later." He scuffed at the grass again.

"I don't think I want to do it," said Mad Martin and Charlie looked somehow relieved at his admission. "I don't either," he agreed. "I think I'd rather do a lot of other interesting things instead of that. Like messing around with cars. Or be a pilot. I'm never going to have any babies."

"I'm supposed to love my grandfather," Mad Martin confided. "But I don't think it has to do with sex."

"Probably not," said Charlie.

Mad Martin closed his eyes and concentrated very hard on his grandfather, conjuring up a picture of Mr. Drivic sitting in the chair in the front room, dozing as the television blared. He waited to see if any kind of feeling came inside him. Nothing happened.

He thought about his grandfather very hard and after a while he could no longer remember. The face dissolved, the features slipped away. It was as if he had never even known a grandfather.

"Come on," Charlie was saying. "It's your go."

Chapter 6

〰〰〰〰〰 It was Saturday. A lady came in with a string bag full of shopping. She sat in the kitchen and drank tea while Mrs. ironed. Mad Martin was standing around on the stairs, trying to get a moment of alone, away from Crimps. He wasn't really listening but the words filtered in through his ears and he heard what they were saying in the kitchen. It was about him.

"What about his parents?" the lady asked Mrs.

"Sssssh," said Mrs. "He never really knew them. Killed outright, they were, in an accident on the motorway."

The lady made clucking sounds and said how he was a poor wee soul.

"You mustn't eavesdrop," Kate said in his ear.

"I wasn't."

"You were. What are you doing if you're not?"

"I'm standing here. I can't help it if I'm listening."

"You could, if you weren't standing here." Kate looked puffed up with importance. She had the acting-like-Mrs. look on her face. She always wore that face when she caught him doing a wrong thing.

"Don't tell," Mad Martin suddenly blurted. It seemed important that she didn't tell he'd heard about his parents. It was the thing he didn't know.

"Well. We can have it for a secret," she told him. "If you like."

52

He didn't want a secret with Kate. He was going to refuse to have a secret but she looked as if she might tell after all. It was his first taste of blackmail. "Okay," he said.

"Good. Now you can come with me."

"Where to?" he asked but she pulled him away to the other room and made him sit at the table where she spread out a board and gave him some discs and told him they were going to play checkers. Mad Martin looked at the board and the pieces and didn't know how to play.

"You don't know anything," Kate said. "But never mind, I'll teach you. Somebody has to teach you."

"Why?" Mad Martin asked, fingering the brown and ivory pieces with his sweaty hands.

"Because. Because otherwise you'll be odd." She peered across the table at him. "You don't want to be odd, do you?"

Mad Martin thought he didn't mind being odd if it meant he didn't know how to play some poxy old game. What he did mind was being told he was odd, and different and wrong and urggy. It seemed to him that odd people could get along quite well if other people weren't always reminding them. It seemed to him that being odd had to do with the other people thinking it about you. For yourself, you were just what you were.

He didn't tell Kate all this. He just said, "Why not?"

Kate was amazed. She gave him a long look down her thin nose. "But you have to know how to play games."

"What for?" he asked her.

"Sportsmanship," she intoned. "If you don't play games, you won't learn how to be a good sport. When you're grown, you'll have to get along with people, won't you? If you haven't learned to be a sport about things when you're small, you won't ever learn it when you're grown."

"Oh," said Mad Martin who couldn't get worked up about being grown, seeing as how it would take such a long time to get there. "So what," he said. "Anyhow, I do know some games. I just don't know this one." That will fix her, he thought, but Kate had an answer for everything.

"Everybody knows how to play checkers," Kate said in her superior stuck up the nose way. "People will think you're very odd if you don't know how. They won't believe you. They'll think you're a snob." She looked at Mad Martin severely, daring him to disagree. Mad Martin looked at the board and wondered at being the only one in the world who didn't know how to play checkers.

"Now then, let's get on with it," she said. With great perseverance, she taught him. But once he grasped the rudiments he felt restless. All this business of hopping around the squares and getting jumped over. Kate had a big stack of almost all his pieces on her side.

"I don't feel like playing anymore," he told her, hoping their secret was not going to be held over his head forever.

"You're not being a good sport," said Kate. "You can't win all the time, you know."

"I haven't even won one time," said Mad Martin. "Anyway, I don't care if I win or not."

"But you do, see. That's why you don't want to play anymore, because you're losing."

Maybe it was true. Now that he thought of it, he could see where it would be more fun if he had all Kate's pieces on his side instead of the other way around. He thought there wasn't much fun in being a good sport. Perhaps he was just a natural bad sport. Anyway, he was fed up with all her lectures and acting like a teacher. He had a teacher in school. One was enough.

"I don't care, anyway, I don't," he said in a sudden fury and felt the lump of hate coming into his throat. He pushed the board hard at Kate, spilling all the pieces in her lap.

"Oooowwww," cried Kate, suddenly as furious as Mad Martin. She began slamming the board up and down on the table and her face got all red.

Mad Martin ran away.

Mrs. Crimp came running from the kitchen wanting to know what was the matter.

"That wasn't very nice, Kate," she said. "Why didn't you let the poor boy win?"

"Mummmmmy," wailed Kate, "you're not supposed to *let* people win. How ever will they learn if you *let* them win?"

"Now Kate," said Mrs. Crimp reasonably, helping to pick up the scattered pieces. "I'm sure it's all right once in a while. It gives them encouragement."

Wronged, Kate wailed louder and had to be shushed and threatened with bed.

Upstairs, Mad Martin allowed himself a gloat. Good, he thought, listening to the din. Serves her right.

Hate, he thought, was far more useful than love. Hate was everywhere, waiting to come out. Love was something you did to make babies and nothing to do with him at all.

So he nourished the hate and found things to do with it. In school. He hadn't planned it but the next time one of the boys kicked him on the stairs Mad Martin heard himself yelling, "I hate you!" It didn't diminish the hurt of the kick but it somehow made him feel better anyway.

The boy who had done the kicking was astounded. He

had been kicking Mad Martin for months, as a matter of course. Mad Martin was good to kick because he never kicked back, or complained, or worse, reported it to a teacher. To tell the truth, it had become a little boring to keep on kicking someone like Mad Martin. The boy was pleased to get a reaction at last.

Thus, Mad Martin's outburst brought him plenty of results. It got him kicked ten times as much as before. He kept on yelling "I hate you" at them. But he didn't think of kicking back.

He felt sure, deep inside, that hate would reap rewards. He waited patiently. Hate was something new and miraculous. It belonged to him. It made him feel unurggy. Hate would never let him down.

Rewards, if they could be called that, did come. Mad Martin developed a jaundiced outlook on the world. He would sit in the bus and when an old lady asked him if he would give her his seat, he wouldn't get up the way he used to. She isn't falling to pieces, he thought. She's sturdy. Let her stand because I'm going to keep on sitting.

He had always let people have their way, he realized now. He always let them get in front of him in the bus queue, for instance, he never made a fuss. Now if someone got in front he pushed and shoved. Hate was strong. Once, when the conductor wouldn't let him on, saying "Full up," he shrieked after the departing bus, "I hate yoooooo," and all the other people left standing with him looked disapproving and shook their heads. Mad Martin gave them all a hateful stare.

The thing was, it made him feel not as good as he thought it would. And he couldn't do it at Crimps, not really. He sensed that Mrs. wouldn't put up with "I hate you's" coming out all the time. That sort of thing wasn't done at Crimps. And anyway, something happened to the hate when he was with them. Instead of getting stronger, it seemed to dwindle as soon as he stepped in the front door. And this was strange, seeing as how the hate had started because of them in the first place.

But in school it came out, more and more. He not only hated the boys but the teacher as well. He stopped writing so diligently in his exercise books. He spent more time looking out the window. If he was asked a question, he answered begrudgingly, not at all like the old Mad Martin who was always willing and polite.

One day at dinnertime, he took his bowl of horrid pud and turned it upside down. Splat, the pudding went on the floor. "Clean it up," he was told as usual but there was a gleam of something different in the teacher's eye. Later he was told to report to the Headmaster.

"Is something troubling you?" the Headmaster wanted to know. With his new powers of observation, Mad Martin observed the Headmaster and took him in. Short, flat face, nose like a carrot, ears with hairs growing out, head like a toothbrush. The Headmaster, heretofore a figure of awe, crumbled in Mad Martin's mumpish eyes.

"It's your grandfather, isn't it?" the Headmaster decided. "I know it must be a difficult time for you," and he talked at length about worrisome changes and how they could up-set a person's life. Who's upset? Not me, Mad Martin thought and held on to his lump of hate, his possession.

But there was that word Love coming into it again. "When someone you love goes away," the Headmaster was saying. Someone you love. Grandfather? Who wanted to hear about all this someone you love? Mad Martin let his eyes roam and eventually they roamed out the window. He let his ears get fogged up and he heard the Headmaster blathering on as if from very far away.

Then for some reason the Headmaster was no longer blathering. He was giving Mad Martin a mournful look. "Are you listening to me?" he asked.

"Oh yes, Sir," said Mad Martin, tearing his eyes away from the window, unstopping his ears in the nick of time.

"I don't think you've been listening to me," the Headmaster said and there was a chill in the air. The Headmaster's nose looked more like a dagger now, poking toward Mad Martin in a dangerous way.

"We've tried to be understanding," he said, not sounding very kindly.

"Yes, Sir," said Mad Martin and he couldn't help dithering his feet.

"But there's a limit to our patience," and the dagger nose made a big jab toward the dithers. Mad Martin ordered his hate to swell up huge and big to protect him. The Headmaster began to threaten. He threatened getting Mrs. Crimp to come to school. Or Mr. Crimp. He threatened how it would do his grandfather no good to have bad reports at a time like this.

"Fighting with the other boys," the Headmaster said, blaming it on Mad Martin.

"But I didn't," Mad Martin said. "I never did fight."

The Headmaster paid no attention. He sent him back to class with a warning.

"We all have to make the best of things," he told him, and he told him to think about his grandfather. "Make him proud of you," he said.

Proud of me, thought Mad Martin on his way back to

class. He didn't know if his grandfather would be bothered with that.

Somewhat subdued, he laid off saying "I hate you" for a while. Mildly alarmed at Mad Martin's visit to the Headmaster's sanctum, the other boys retreated a safe distance to see if there would be repercussions. On both sides, there was a kind of truce.

"I don't know," Mad Martin said to Charlie when they were in bed. It had become their time to have talks. "I don't know. This hate thing is getting me down."

"Oh?" Charlie said, alerted. He had come to understand he must be prepared to answer explicitly whenever Mad Martin wanted information. He often felt it was like an exam.

"This thing of *really* hating. I don't know whether I like it."

Ha, ha, laughed Charlie. "Maybe you hate it."

Mad Martin was in no mood for jokes. "Yeah, maybe I do," he said. He hated hating. Now where was he?

"You're not supposed to like hating," said Charlie, sounding like Kate. "It makes you mean and ugly."

"What?" Mad Martin exclaimed, feeling frightened.

"It turns you horrible," Charlie went on. "You get all filled up with hate and it comes leaking out. You become a mess. Nobody likes you. Actually, you're supposed to do more loving than hating if you really want to know."

Mad Martin felt in a turmoil. "Why didn't you tell me before?" he cried. "You said it was okay, that it wasn't a disease."

"Oh it's not a disease," explained Charlie. "I mean, it's not contagious or anything like that. I don't think you can die from it."

"I don't get it," Mad Martin said, sullen now, in danger of having a repercussion of hate. "I don't know what I'm supposed to love. I mean, they tell me what sometimes . . . but I don't get how you go about doing it." Sullenness was dissolving into wretchedness.

Charlie thought awhile. Yawned, because these discussions were very tiring. He wished this Martin would want to talk about things like planes and cars and stuff. Nobody else he knew ever asked all these queer questions. But his parents had explained that the boys they took into care were sometimes a bit dotty, only you weren't supposed to call it that. They had problems, like from broken homes or terrible tragedies. He had been told he must try to understand, seeing as he was so lucky not to have the tragedies himself, as his mum said.

"Maybe," he advised, stifling yawns, "you should ask your grandad if you can get a dog." It was obvious to Charlie that dogs were one of the best sorts of things to love.

"Yeah, well," said Mad Martin dubiously, "but that still doesn't tell me how I'm supposed to get this love."

"Never mind," yawned Charlie. "You'll find out sooner or later, I expect."

Mad Martin had his doubts.

Chapter 7

With the hate and love business messed up in his mind, Mad Martin decided he would feel nothing for a while. He pined for the days when it was always the same sameness and he had never been bothered with feelings. He got out his diary, sorely neglected since he had come to Crimps and been overpowered by them, and flipped through the empty pages. I'll just write down the usuals, he thought, and never mind about hating or loving. He got his pencil and wrote the date and began: "I got up. I put my pajamas in the wash because it's washday. Charlie and me had fooling around time before we got dressed for school. We threw things until Mrs. yelled that's enough. I got dressed. I ate my breakfast. Susan spilled milk all over the table and screamed it was John's fault. John and Mark punched each other. Mr. Crimp said he wanted peace and quiet when he ate. Mrs. slapped Mark and John. I went to school."

Mad Martin stopped writing, astonished that he had already filled a whole page and had only got up to the point of going to school. He had meant to write only the usuals but it seemed that at Crimps, the usuals took up far more space than they did at home. At this rate, his diary would be filled up in no time and he would have to find a way to get another book. *Just* the *usuals*, he reminded himself and continued writing, not liking to leave an entry undone: "I came back from school. I had my tea. Charlie and me had a kick around in the yard. I hit the target twice and Charlie said I improved. He said next door, Mrs. Thingie was pregs, is what she called having a baby and she told Mrs. it was bad luck because she already got three. Charlie must be wrong about special love being babies because if it was then it wouldn't be bad luck would it?" Once again, Mad Martin stopped writing and was disheartened to see the usuals had taken up yet another full page. Two pages and he wasn't even finished with the day! He used to be able to get two or three days on one page. I'll rub it out, he thought, all the not-usual stuff. But reading it over, it all seemed usual, it all seemed important. What was wrong?

"We had supper. I went to bed," he wrote decisively and against his principles because he had not yet actually had supper or gone to bed.

"What're you doing?" Charlie asked, coming into the bedroom where Mad Martin was sitting on the floor with his diary in his lap.

"Nothing," said Mad Martin and put the book away with his small hoard of belongings in one of the drawers that had been allotted to him.

"Sorry," said Charlie who had been taught not to pry and could sometimes overcome the temptation. He was wearing his new glasses, presented to him with dire threats by Mrs. should he break the frames again. Seeing that Mad Martin was now empty-handed he asked, "Want to do something?" and sniffled his glasses up and down his nose.

"You look like a pig when you do that," said Mad Martin. It just came out. As soon as he said it he felt panicky, wondering what Charlie would think.

Charlie laughed. He did it some more, making himself look even more piglike and he oinked all over the room. Oink, oink, oink. "Ugh," he said, taking the glasses off and throwing them down on the bed and almost sitting on them. "I hate them."

Mad Martin, much more sophisticated now, knew it was an insignificant hate. Hating glasses was like hating puddings.

"Let's do something," Charlie said.

"What then?" asked Mad Martin, thinking about how he had told Charlie he had looked like a pig and got away with it.

"I don't know, something, let's go out in the street."

Mad Martin knew Mrs. didn't like that. She said you played in the back garden which is what she called the yard or you played in the park but not in the road like guttersnipes. "I don't know," he said.

They thought a bit, in silence.

"Well what should we do?" asked Mad Martin.

"You think of something for a change," Charlie replied.

"Me?"

"I'm always doing the thinking of what to do. What did you do when you were home? Give us an idea for a change."

Mad Martin thought. At home, he did the usually usual which took up a lot less space in his diary than what went on around here. "Ohh," Mad Martin said. "Well," he said. "Ummm." He didn't do nothing at home and it had always seemed okay.

"You know what?" Charlie said suddenly.

"What?"

"You're a right drip." The way he said it stung Mad

Martin. He had been called lots of names in school but coming from Charlie a name was newly painful. Names seemed a part of school but here it was in Charlie's room with Charlie saying it. Mad Martin felt hurt and angry and wanted to say something back. Summoning the only defense he knew, culled from his education at Crimp hands, he shouted, "You shouldn't say that, it's rude."

Charlie only shrugged. "I tell you what, let's go to the canal."

"I'm not going," said Mad Martin, pouting and turning away.

"Oink, oink," said Charlie. "That's rude as well, calling people pigs."

"I didn't."

"You did."

"I never said you were a pig."

"Said I looked like one," Charlie retorted hotly. But then he simmered down. "Anyway, I'm not angry. Are you going to be a baby or what? Let's go to the canal."

So you really don't get away with it, Mad Martin thought. You could tell somebody something insulting but you had to get told something insulting back. If they didn't get angry, you couldn't either. Yes, that was the way it was. Satisfied with the logic of things, Mad Martin agreed to go.

"But we'll have to not say we're going," said Charlie. "We'll say we're going to the shops for a comic."

Mad Martin noticed Charlie fidgeting with his glasses. "Listen," he said, thinking to make things better, "you don't really look like a pig."

But instead of putting the glasses on his head, Charlie stuffed them into his shirt pocket.

"You come home in time," warned Mrs. "Don't you go loitering and make yourselves late."

The canal could be a stinky place in parts. But mostly it was lovely. The water meandered sluggishly, brown and green and black. They walked along the towpath and time disappeared. They skittered stones and poked with sticks. They got mud on their shoes and didn't care. Mad Martin wondered why he had never before discovered the joys of this wet, lonely world. It was as if they were thousands of miles away from schools or home or suppers. It was a place unencumbered by everythings. It simply existed. It was like the blanks in his mind coming to life and he knew now that the blanks were times when he must have wanted to be somewhere like this.

They walked and walked, forgetting the admonitions about being late, and came upon a group of boys who were pushing themselves back and forth across the murky waters on a flat, makeshift barge.

Mad Martin could have done without the boys, they were like an imposition on his discovery and his quiet oneness with Charlie. But Charlie was excited, waving and shouting, asking if they could come on for a ride.

"Nawww," the boys shouted back unpleasantly and Mad Martin thought, Good, now we'll be on our way to where it's quiet again. But Charlie was insisting.

"Maybe," they called back this time. Mad Martin twitched at Charlie's sleeve. "Come on," he said, "let's go."

"No look," Charlie said, all agog at the possibility of getting on the barge. "They're coming over for us."

Mad Martin hung back, watching as Charlie made a deal

with them. If he'd been alone he would have avoided the boys because they would have been sure to trip him up or thump him but Charlie was able to talk to them, like all talking Crimps, with convincing logic until the boys were worn down and said they could come on for a ride. Already great friends, Charlie waved Mad Martin to join them.

"Who's he?" they wanted to know, as if they had known Charlie all their lives.

"Him? He's Martin," said Charlie. Then they were on the barge and the boys were pushing with the poles and they were soon in the middle of the canal and the water was lapping up on all sides in a black, threatening way. Mad Martin thought how he'd only swum in bathtubs, not ever in water deep as this.

Not satisfied with just having a ride, Charlie wanted to pole and there was a fracas then, with the boys shouting orders and Mad Martin being pushed out of the way and the barge swaying crazily.

And then Charlie fell in.

Mad Martin watched Charlie sink, mesmerized by the solid swift way the body bubbled down and his first lowly thought was that he was glad it wasn't himself sinking, and his second thought was what would Mrs. say and only third and finally did he wonder in sudden fright if Charlie could swim. But then there was a great thrashing and churning and Charlie's head appeared, hair plastered down like glue, mouth spitting water, and all the other boys, having momentarily been as paralyzed as Mad Martin, sprang into action.

They were helpful but not sympathetic and totally unconcerned over the state of Charlie's clothes or the squelches in his shoes. "Gosh, they stayed on" was all Charlie could sputter as he was hauled over the edge of the barge and he launched into a nervous and lengthy discourse about how shoes always came off and sank when a person fell overboard. The boys stared at Charlie's shoes and then at his soaking face like he was some smarmy loony. And while all this was going on Mad Martin happened to notice that Charlie's glasses were floating gently downstream.

This time Mad Martin was not mesmerized. He quickly lay flat out on the barge and reached for the glasses and when he could not get a grip on them, he stretched himself farther and just as he had them in his clutches he felt himself slip and in he went with a small unobserved plop.

It was not so bad drowning. He could see everything fine and clear and he could breathe fine and he still held the glasses in his hand. Not wanting his drowning to be for nothing, he carefully maneuvered them into his pocket, the one with the button on, although he couldn't quite manage to do up the button again under the water as he was. He thought, they'll find them when they dredge up my body and this made him feel happy and then he felt a sharp pain in his back and something like maybe a fish biting him all over and then the terrible shock of being undrowned and alive again.

They dumped him on the deck unceremoniously. Only Charlie was concerned. It was not so easy to breathe now and as Mad Martin coughed and choked he thought he would have done better to remain underwater.

"Couple of bathing beauties, they are," the boys said, plainly disgusted and kicked them off the barge as unseaworthy. Charlie and Mad Martin stood on the bank and dripped.

"Oh gosh, what'll we do?" Charlie asked plaintively.

Mad Martin was still choking up canal water.

"We won't half get it," Charlie moaned, trying to wring out his trousers.

"Drowning's okay," said Mad Martin, full of the knowledge of it and heaving up the last of the chokes, "as long as you don't get saved."

Charlie began shivering and, like a disease, Mad Martin caught it from him.

"I'm not going home, that's for sure," Charlie said, clicking teeth.

"We'll dry out," chattered Mad Martin, blasé now that he had survived.

"We won't. Not in time. Besides, look at the muck on us."

"Oh," said Mad Martin, feeling less blasé. He knew how Mrs. went on about dirty clothes. But seeing Charlie, his mentor, so disheveled and hopeless, he felt he must grope around in his mind for some comforting idea.

"She'll be glad we're not dead, your mum," he offered.

"Oh belt up," said Charlie, giving him a look as he tried to rub the mud off his shirt. He sat down on the bank with a squish.

Mad Martin felt very cold and horrible. It was all right being wet in the water but not so good when you were out of it and standing in your clothes. He sat down next to Charlie and meticulously picked out the knots in his shoelaces. It was hard to untie them wet. When he got them undone at last, he poured the water out of his shoes, despondently counting the drops until there were no more.

He hoped Charlie would get an idea. But Charlie sat there.

"Oh well," said Mad Martin, putting his shoes back on again. His socks felt all slimy going back in.

"I'm not going, that's it," said Charlie.

Mad Martin didn't think it would be much fun spending a whole night by the side of the canal, stinky and lovely though it was. Personally, he was all for going back, rage of Mrs. and all. But it was Charlie's house, he couldn't just go without him. On the other hand, his untrustworthy and devious stomach was craving all the everythings they would be having for supper. There was nothing he could do with better now than food and bed. Maybe Mrs. would give them hot-water bottles. Mrs. had a whole cupboard full of bottles. He never thought he'd see the day when he would be pining for Crimps but the trouble was he had grown accustomed to their style of life. He didn't want it all to disappear just because he fell in the canal.

"Here, look," he said, jabbing Charlie in the wet ribs with enthusiasm. "Let's go to my house first."

"Eh?" said Charlie, looking more miserable than ever.

"My house. We can go there and dry off."

"What d'you mean, *your* house?" Charlie wanted to know.

"My house, that's what I mean. I got a key and we can get in and put the fire on and get dried and then Mrs., I mean your mum, won't know what happened."

Mad Martin was gratified to see that Charlie's eye began to look alive again, less soggy.

"Yeah?" said Charlie. "Yeah!"

So they went. Mad Martin felt good that he could show the way and do something important for Charlie. The tables were turned. It wasn't him, Mad Martin, who was having to grope and find his way about how to do things. It was Charlie at a loss and urggy old Mad Martin showing him how!

But he didn't let it go to his head either. He had heard Mrs. telling them often enough, Pride goeth before a fall, fond as she was of thinking up quotes from scriptures. Pride going before a fall meant getting cocky and high and mighty and coming down with a bump when you found out you weren't so grand as you thought.

Now he had the opportunity of doing something good and wonderful and he was careful not to look too proud when he took the key out of its hiding hole and opened the front door of his house.

"Please come in," he said, as he had learned at Crimps, and Charlie stepped over the threshold and looked around and then came the fall because Mad Martin had forgotten how his own house was full of nothing and Charlie's full of everything. He felt miserable watching Charlie looking at the front room with its two chairs and table instead of bookshelves, lamps and cushions and pictures and the sewing machine which was the contraption Mrs. kept in the corner.

"It's not very swank," Mad Martin said.

"It's okay," said Charlie. "Where's the fire then?" and he was already stripping off his wet clothes, not at all put off by the lack of everythings.

Dutifully, Mad Martin switched the fire on and held his breath until he saw the coils getting red, afraid the electricity might have been shut off.

"Oooh, that's better," said Charlie, still shivering.

"We could have some tea to warm us," said Mad Martin enthusiastically, "only we got no milk," he finished, lame.

"We could have cocoa instead," said Charlie.

"Yes but we don't have milk," Mad Martin said once more, understanding how difficult it was to convince someone who always had everything that you didn't have nothing.

70

"Let's get some. Is there a shop?" Charlie was searching his trousers. The glasses, Mad Martin thought, I must tell him. But Charlie was then exclaiming as he found his pocket money still wrapped in its wad of handkerchief deep down inside the murky pocket.

"Should I go?" Mad Martin asked, feeling awkward about letting the neighbors see him. There was no hope for it, he had to go because Charlie already had his trousers off. "I know where it is," and he took the money and ran out and hoped Charlie wouldn't be afraid staying in the house alone. But when he came back with the pint of milk and the cheapest packet of cocoa he could find, Charlie was comfortably ensconced in one of the chairs with his legs getting grilled, not looking frightened of anything.

"I'll make it," Mad Martin said, as much to play host as to keep Charlie out of the kitchen which would surely shock him in its impoverished state of neglect. Because now Mad Martin noticed things like that and could make comparisons. He felt momentarily faint at heart when he realized Charlie would have to come through the kitchen to get to the loo and he floundered between pouring the milk into the pan and thinking of pouring some of the disinfectant stuff down the toilet as Mrs. and the other lady had done that first day they came. Crimp toilets never smelled bad. Mad Martin was now aware that his did.

As he waited for the milk to heat up, he took a few swipes at the crusty old worktop with a rag. The rag was dirtier than the worktop. Spots and stains leapt out from everywhere. There was a whole mountain of crumbs under the breadboard. Mrs. didn't allow crumbs to collect. She swept them away after every bread cutting and wiped the board clean. Hers had no greasy butter spots or coagulated marmalade lumps on it. Mad Martin rubbed at the lumps and finally picked one or two off with his fingernail. It didn't make much difference, there were hundreds more. Hundreds of faults and urgginesses all over the kitchen. "Oh who cares anyway," said Mad Martin as the milk began boiling over. He threw in several big spoons of cocoa, stirred, and then was in agony again over the cups. He'd better have the one with the crack in it. But what about saucers? The cups looked bare without saucers; he'd got used to saucers at Crimps. Who cares, who cares, he chanted to himself as he brought the two steaming cups into the front room. Charlie was now toasting his back.

"Thanks," he said as he took a cup. Mad Martin watched anxiously for complaints before he could relax enough to enjoy his own.

"It would be nice to stay here forever," Charlie said un-expectedly. "It's like my camp, only better. We could camp here and no one would find us. It would be our se-cret place."

Crimps were mad for secrets but this one Mad Martin could definitely share. Yes it would be lovely, him and Charlie, living together in the house, drinking cocoa and getting the milk delivered again. They wouldn't even bother with school and Charlie could have Grandfather's bed and . . . Mad Martin stopped, drawn up short at the brick wall of his grandfather. That would spoil it. Almost, almost, he wished his grandfather wouldn't come back from hospital. Maybe his damaged hip would stay damaged for-ever. Maybe, even, he would die.

After he thought this, about his grandfather dying, he felt funny in the head and was glad when Charlie dropped the subject of secret camps and said, "You could have a dog here, easy."

"We had a cat but she got run over by a car," Mad Martin told him.

"Cats are no good. It's best to have a dog. They only *chase* cars, not get run down by them."

"I like dogs," observed Mad Martin. There were several dogs living on Mop Street and except for the nuisance of stepping in their messes on the pavement once in a while, they seemed affable creatures. But some of them were quite a size. "Do you think dogs eat much?" he asked.

"Depends," said Charlie. "Get a medium one and it won't be too bad."

"Oh," said Mad Martin, digesting this information. "How about a small one? They would eat even less."

"Not too small," cautioned Charlie. "Too small and they get yappy. You want a medium one so it can be a watchdog. Burglars step on small ones. A big one is best," Charlie said wistfully. "But they eat you out of house and home, my mum says."

"I'd get a medium one then," said Mad Martin.

"Could you? Will your grandad let you?" Charlie was very interested, excited.

"I'd have to ask. I expect he wouldn't mind a pet. He liked the cat all right. I think." Yes, his grandfather did like the cat because once he went to call the cat in and just then remembered she was squashed. Then didn't he seem sad? Sadder than Mad Martin had previously thought. "The poor mačka," he said, and Mad Martin had wanted to ask a question about it but he knew his grandfather was not in the mood.

"Oh do ask him. Promise you will!" said Charlie. "You could write him a letter."

"Oh no," said Mad Martin who had never written a letter to anybody in his life.

"Well ask him when he comes home then. Don't forget," Charlie kept on about it.

"Maybe," said Mad Martin, not liking the way Charlie was insisting. After all, whose dog was it going to be?

"Why don't *you* get a dog?" he asked Charlie.

Charlie looked down at the floor and wriggled his bare red toes. "I can't," he said.

"Why not?" It didn't make sense seeing as how Charlie was so daft about dogs.

"Because of the carpets, see," said Charlie. "It would mess on the carpets and get dog hairs in the Hoover and make it smell bad like Mrs. Thingie's next door. My mum says their place smells of dog and you can't ever get rid of it."

Looking at his own carpetless floors, Mad Martin understood. He didn't know whether to feel glad or angry. He had something Charlie didn't, unbelievable but true. No carpets. Charlie was envious. But then, Charlie didn't think a dog smell would make much difference here, and that wasn't so nice, was it?

Mad Martin decided not to feel angry. He could afford to act grand because he had a place suitable for dogs whereas Charlie was encumbered with his bothersome carpets. Obviously, having lots of everything was not always practical.

"I think I will get a dog," he said grandly.

But instead of giving envious congratulations, Charlie turned sulky. "We won't half get it anyway, dry as we are and all. We better go home."

Mad Martin agreed half-heartedly. He wasn't looking forward to what Mrs. would have to say.

Their clothes were dry all right but stiff as boards. Their shoes were still sodden and smelled of heated-up feet. Charlie got dressed and Mad Martin collected the cups and turned off the fire. Thankfully, Charlie did not want to use the loo or have a tour of the upper rooms. They locked the door, returned the key to its hiding place and went off. They had no more money and had to walk and it took longer than the bus and even Charlie made a muddle getting them to go the right way. It was very late when they got back to Crimps.

All the lights were blazing. Even before they could ring the bell, the door was thrown open and loud exclamations ensued. Mad Martin hung back, terrified, and let Charlie get the brunt of it. But Mrs. spied him cowering and then he was included too. Mrs. was like a tall volcano, exploding words at the top. The words showered down, hot and blazing, beating them on their muddy heads. Mr. Crimp joined in but in a quieter way. He said Mrs. had been worried about them, thinking they'd come to harm. Mad Martin thought it was a peculiar way to act worried. He thought Mrs. ought to be smiling and glad instead of making such a row. His grandfather never made rows about coming home late. But then, his grandfather didn't seem to get worried either. Thinking about it, it occurred to Mad Martin that his grandfather didn't really notice whether he was there or not. Anyway, they never had schedules like Crimps had. Mrs. liked everything to happen on the proper dot.

Finally, it calmed down. Mrs. stopped exploding and said they better both have baths. Mad Martin let himself have a small think about whether they might get to have some supper after the baths.

And then Mrs. started on about the glasses.

"And where are your glasses?" Mrs. asked Charlie who wasn't wearing them.

"Grrreek," said Charlie, feeling his empty nose.

"You've lost your glasses," said Mrs. sounding like doom.

"I didn't," said Charlie, peering into his empty shirt pocket.

"Where are they then?" asked Mrs. and Mad Martin marveled at how Charlie's face could look so many different ways so fast: blank, remembering, horrified, scared and green. "Lost," said Mrs. ominously.

"I'm glad," Charlie shouted. "They're bloody awful. They make me look like a pig."

Mad Martin, in the process of removing the lost glasses from his pocket, was shocked. He felt very sorry about that pig business, he did. He had never expected it to come up again, especially at a time like this. He had been about to save the day, whipping out the glasses to show they were found and hoping to create cheerful happiness all around so they could get on with the poxy baths and at last get some proper supper. The cocoa was slopping around in his empty stomach something terrible.

"I have them," he said quietly.

Mrs. looked huffy and snatched them away to inspect for damage.

Charlie wouldn't look at him at all. He didn't even say thanks.

Things were simpler on Mop Street, Mad Martin thought. Out in the world of people, you never knew how they were going to act next. It gave him knots in his brain. His grandfather had acted only one way: the same.

Chapter 8

One day Mrs. announced that Mad Martin was going to be taken to visit his grandfather in a nursing home. He was out of hospital now, and recuperating. It sounded as if his grandfather was recuperating from the hospital. Perhaps it had been an ordeal and his grandfather had suffered. Mad Martin tried to connect the idea of his grandfather suffering to some feeling inside himself but nothing happened. The old blankness dwelled inside him regardless of all the Crimps hollering about how he must be missing, loving, pining for his grandad.

Everyone was very excited about the visit, although it wasn't *their* grandfather. Mad Martin wasn't excited. He felt funny. He thought he could jolly well do without a visit.

But there was Mrs. making all the hustle and bustle again, getting him ready and presentable. Making sure he had his bath. Making sure about clean clothes. Making sure he didn't go out in the garden and get muck all over his trousers just when she had him fixed up so nice.

"What's it matter anyway?" Mad Martin grumbled.

"What does it matter?" exclaimed Mrs., throwing her hands up to her hair which was fixed all fancy for the trip. "You want to look nice for your grandad, don't you?"

"He won't notice nothing," said Mad Martin. That was

the difference between Mrs. and Grandfather. Mrs. was always concerned about looking nice for things. Special clothes for special occasions. At home it was the same clothes for everything, his grandfather was only interested if you put on your coat when it was cold and took it off again when it was hot.

"What will people think of you," Mrs. said, "if you don't take a bit of trouble over your appearance?"

Mad Martin wasn't used to thinking what people thought of him. "I don't care," he said.

"Well, I do!" said Mrs. emphatically. This puzzled Mad Martin. Perhaps if he looked urggy, they would think Mrs. was urggy too.

Mrs. tried to explain why looking nice was important. On the way to the nursing home she told him, "Look around and see for yourself. Look at how people are dressed and think about what you think of them. If you see a shabby person, do you feel the same as you do when someone's nicely dressed?"

Mad Martin looked around. "Maybe they're poor," he said.

"Well yes." Mrs. was forced to admit this might be true. "But I mean to say, a dirty person. Someone who just doesn't care."

Mad Martin walked on, looking for a dirty person. He thought about Shirley lying squashed and messy in the gutter. "The person is inside," he told Mrs. "Why does it matter what's on the outside covering the body up?"

"Oh dear," said Mrs., looking puzzled herself. "You're perfectly right of course. But it's just that people often act the way they look. If someone doesn't care if he looks filthy, he probably won't care if he acts filthy as well." Mrs.

meditated as they waited for the traffic light to change. "No matter what your circumstances," she said firmly, as they crossed the street, "you can always wash your hands and face and try to look nice."

"I still don't see exactly why," said Mad Martin doggedly, wondering if a soul had to wash its hands and face and look nice.

But Mrs. was getting cross. "It's done, that's all," she said. "Most people think it's right. Making a good impression is half the battle in life, I'm sorry to say." It was the first time Mad Martin had heard that life was a battle. He wanted to think about this but Mrs. kept on talking. "People judge a book by its cover," she was saying. "I'm afraid they don't often trouble themselves to look inside. Do you see what I mean, Martin? There's no sense not trying a little to make a good impression."

Mad Martin thought it wasn't so bad having a conversation with Mrs., private like this, it wasn't half bad, it wasn't. Much better than having a conversation with the Headmaster, for instance. And much better than having a conversation with Kate.

"Why," he asked, "do people want to make impressions?" He wasn't too sure about that word. Was it like pressing on a bit of mud with your shoe, making an impression of your heel? He didn't see how people could do that to each other, a body wasn't like mud, you could get close but you couldn't leave any marks of yourself behind. Probably it was brains. The thoughts made heel-marks in people's brains.

"To get ahead in life," was Mrs.'s answer. She clutched her purse and clamped it against her ample stomach. "Now stop asking and come along," she said.

Walking beside Mrs., Mad Martin wondered if he was making a good impression on all the people they passed. About getting ahead in life, he didn't know. He supposed he would get ahead in life regardless, seeing as how he got older every year.

He would have liked to ask Mrs. another question but he could see she was in no mood. It had to do about the insides of a person. You could wash up and be all nice but what if you weren't so nice inside? Like Charlie said about hate making you ugly. If you were full of hate and ugly, then no amount of washing and baths was going to change it. And what about an ugly who couldn't help it? Like somebody born that way? He'd seen a man on a bus with a big purple mark all over his face. His grandfather had called it a birthmark. The man with the birthmark should be allowed to make a good impression too. He could wash his face every day and never get it off. It shouldn't be held against him. Insides were important too, Mad Martin thought.

The nursing home looked mild on the outside, what with hedges and flowers growing and looking like somebody's cottage in a fairytale book. But inside it was an overpowering place. There were glass walls and desks and ladies in uniforms with watches pinned on their chests. Mad Martin felt dwindled. He stayed close to Mrs. Crimp's large skirt, glad to have her there.

When one of the uniforms said, "Oh yes, Mr. Drivic," Mad Martin got an attack of butterflies. No, he wanted to say as Mrs. took his hand and started pulling in the direction of a long corridor. He didn't say it. It would be a loony thing to say now that he was already here. He was supposed to be feeling excited and happy, as all Crimps kept telling him. Excited maybe yes but he didn't know about happy. Yuuuunnyuuunnyunnn, went all the butterflies, smashing around inside his guts. His legs felt all wobbly. I'm scared, thought Mad Martin, trying to conjure up a vision of his grandfather. All he could imagine was a faceless character wrapped in bandages.

But when they came into a large room, there were very few bandages. Men in beds, all covered up with sheets and only the heads sticking out. Mad Martin looked around, petrified, certain he would never be able to recognize his grandfather among all those heads. The nurse lady was leading them and Mrs. was dragging him and they came to a bed with a big hump in it, like somebody might be hiding under the sheets. There he was, face-to-face, his grandfather looking at him and him looking back. He recognized him after all. The butterflies abated only slightly.

Mrs. gave a big booming "Hullo, Mr. Drivic," and Mad Martin was relieved when his grandfather didn't boom back. "Hello," his grandfather said quietly. "Zdravo," he said to Mad Martin, with a queer smile around his pale old lips.

"Zdravo," Mad Martin whispered, feeling embarrassed to say it and also peculiar about seeing his grandfather in a nightdress with his stringy neck all prickly and sticking out like a turtle.

Mrs. made a conversation, as was her ability, and Mad Martin let them get on with it, happy not to have to think up something to say. But then before he knew it came his turn, Mrs. sort of prodding him in his back and his grandfather looking somehow expectant. What was he going to say, and with Mrs. there listening to every word?

"Have you been a good boy?" his grandfather asked.

"Yes," said Mad Martin, wondering if Mrs. would deny it.

But Mrs. was taking things out of her carrying bag, presents, she said, for Mr. Drivic. Mad Martin watched her, his mind gone blank.

"My grandson," Mr. Drivic said suddenly.

"What's that? Your grandson?" The man in the next bed hitched himself up to get a better look. "A fine boy," he said. "A fine boy." He hitched higher. "Your grandad's been telling me all about you. He's proud of you. I hope you've been keeping up the good work."

Mad Martin didn't know what to say. What good work? And there was his grandfather looking him over with an expression that must mean he was proud. There was his grandfather noticing how nice he looked and being proud that somebody else thought so too.

"I brought you a few things, Mr. Drivic," Mrs. said as she unloaded a mound of apples onto the bedside table.

Mr. Drivic stared at the apples. "No good," he said. "My teeth." He opened his mouth and pointed. "No teeth for eating apples."

"Oh my, I didn't think," said Mrs., uneasy at having to look into Mr. Drivic's mouth. Mad Martin expected his grandfather to be cross now, annoyed, like he sometimes was when something didn't go exactly right. His grandfather didn't like to be bothered too much. He would think Mrs. was being a nosy neighbor bringing him apples when he couldn't bite them. But instead his grandfather was doing a strange thing. He was laughing. Out loud. It was shaking his face and his neck and even his shoulders that looked so funny in the nightdress. "Never mind, never mind," he said to Mrs. "I can cut them with a knife. Thanks."

82

Mrs. was laughing now too. And the man in the other bed. Mad Martin didn't laugh. He wished his grandfather hadn't opened his mouth and shown Mrs. all his horrid old broken teeth. Mrs. liked only clean white teeth that were brushed with a toothbrush. She might be laughing now but sooner or later she would start in telling Mr. Drivic that his teeth were urggy.

"And so what did you bring for your grandad?" the man in the other bed wanted to know. He was nosy all right. He fixed his nosy old eyes right on Mad Martin and waited for an answer.

"I don't know," said Mad Martin, full of sudden terror. "I just brought myself I guess."

"Not bad," the man said.

"Yes, it's good," said Mr. Drivic. "It's fine. That's all I want, to see my little unuk, my grandson."

This made Martin feel teary and odd. He couldn't look at his grandfather's face. He looked down at the floor and hoped the bumpy lump in his throat would go away quick.

"Well, what have you been up to, eh?" Mr. Drivic asked Mad Martin.

Mad Martin's mind became a jumble, everything he had been up to was in a heap, impossible to straighten out and talk about.

"I fell in the canal," he blurted. Mrs. gave a little start and made a noise.

"I didn't drown," he said. "I wasn't afraid either."

"I should think not," said the other bed. "A boy your size!"

Mad Martin felt a little deflated.

"That's all, falling in the canal?" his grandfather said and did that laughing business again.

"Uh," said Mad Martin, wishing the other bed wasn't listening to every word. "I play football." He didn't like having to do all this talking about himself. If they were home, his grandfather and him, they wouldn't be doing all this talking about what he'd been up to. His grandfather was never interested in that kind of stuff before. He wished they would all stop looking at him and expecting him to talk. It was like when he was first at Crimps, with Charlie and Kate and Mark and John all asking him, wanting him to tell them things. He put a hand out and nervously touched the big hump in the bed. "What's this?" he asked.

Ha, ha, his grandfather laughed sadly. "That's my hip. I'm broken down, good for nothing."

"Pay him no mind," the other bed ordered. "Broken down, my eye! He's up and around and chasing the nurses." He leaned toward Mad Martin confidentially. "He'll be running in the Olympics next year, your grandad." Mad Martin stepped backward to get away from the smell of medicine breath. But the man was holding out his hand. "My name's Davies," he said. "How do you do?" He reached under his sheets and rummaged and brought out a bunch of grapes. "Here, have a grape."

Mrs. looked askance at grapes that came from under bed sheets. She hustled Mad Martin around to the other side of his grandfather's bed. "Why don't you two have a visit?" she suggested. "I'll just have a look round outside." She left Mad Martin standing there, tongue-tied.

"They treating you okay?" his grandfather asked.

Mad Martin nodded.

"Any complaints?"

Mad Martin shook his head.

"Doesn't have much to say for himself, does he?" Mr. Davies nosed in.

Mr. Drivic made the na-na sound, as if to tell Mr. Davies to mind his own business but Mr. Davies kept right on.

"Doesn't take after his grandfather, does he?" he said. "Your grandad," he told Mad Martin, "talks more than all of us put together. Tells us stories. He'd keep on all night with those stories but the nurse won't let him. My word, what a life your grandad's had. Ah but you've heard all about it, haven't you?"

Mad Martin gaped. What kind of stories could his grandfather be telling? His grandfather had never told him any stories. Mr. Davies, that nosy parker, must be making it up.

"Did he ever tell you the one about stealing the goat?" Mr. Davies rattled on. "Or how he tried to sneak on the ship and be a stowaway? Oh that was a good one!" Mr. Davies chuckled and snorted and had a coughing fit. Instead of telling him to stop his nosy lies, Mr. Drivic just sat there looking pleased.

Mad Martin felt miles away from pleased. He felt shrieky inside. Like he wanted to yell and maybe cry. It was this stupid nursing home, that was what was the matter. It made everything wonko. Why, his grandfather didn't even look like himself anymore. Sitting in the bed with that stupid nightdress on. All happy, he was. Like he had never been on Mop Street. Like he had never even heard of Mop Street.

Could've told *me* some of them stories, Mad Martin thought. Not that I believe it.

He was glad that Mrs. came back just then. The presence of Mrs. made things seem more normal, less bunged up.

"Kiss your grandad goodbye," she said. Mad Martin wanted to faint. He never kissed his grandfather, goodbye or hello or anything.

Lucky thing his grandfather only patted his head. But even so, Mad Martin felt himself shrinking away from the touch. To make up for it, he whispered "Zbògom." His grandfather smiled, showing stubbly old teeth again. Mr. Davies waved.

He moped on the journey back, making Mrs. ask what was wrong with him and couldn't he pick up his feet?

"I should think you'd be delighted," she said, "seeing your grandad looking so well and knowing it won't be long before you can go home."

They're fed up taking care of me, Mad Martin thought and this made him uneasy. All this time at Crimps, he had been thinking that all he wanted to do was go home but now it seemed different. His grandfather was a stranger, turned strange by the hospital. What would it be like at home now? It might be good if he could hear some of those famous stories but it would probably be the same as before which should have made him glad but it didn't.

Home. A silent place with bare floors. "Where's my slipper?" and "Time for bed." Better than Crimps with all that lot of blab going on all the time. Yes, much better. Just as long as his grandfather would be back to his old self.

But for some reason, this gave Mad Martin a hollow feeling. He felt lonesome when he thought of it. He'd forgotten to ask about the dog. A dog would be less lonesome. Maybe.

"I said, isn't it nice you'll soon be going home?" Mrs. was saying but he hadn't been listening.

Home with nobody to hate and no problems about love. All the clutter put in his brain by Crimps. Washing machines and blue-and-white egg cups, pillows and books and pictures and carpets. All the everythings that now seemed to be reaching out like a big claw, threatening to tear him to pieces before it would let him go. Mad Martin felt dizzy.

"Yes," he said, stopping a moment to get his breath and equilibrium back. "It's best if I can go home soon."

"What a funny boy you are," said Mrs., getting out her key. "I thought you liked it here with us."

Such was the mystery of Mrs. and the way she could think.

Chapter 9

〰〰〰〰〰〰 There was a big commotion going on one Saturday afternoon not long after the visit to the nursing home. Mad Martin was upstairs in Charlie's room writing in the diary which was almost used up. Charlie was out having football practice with his school team, and Mad Martin had successfully escaped from Kate.

He heard all the noise downstairs and came out to see what was going on. There was Mark standing in the front room, wailing. There was Mrs. inspecting for damages and Kate was giving unwanted advice. Mr. Crimp was chuckling.

"Well, I hope you gave him a run for his money," he said to Mark.

"He stole my ball and ran off," said Mark, still wailing and sobbing.

"And what did you do?" asked Mr. Crimp.

"Nothing. He was bigger."

"You have to learn to stand up for yourself, my boy," said Mr. Crimp, no longer chuckling.

"He kicked me," cried Mark, hoisting a trouser leg. "See, here, look." Mr. Crimp was not impressed. "Crying like a baby is not the answer," he said. Mrs. came in with a wet cloth and tried to wash Mark's face.

"Will you get it back, Dad?" asked Mark. "He's in the park, can you go and make him give it back?"

Mr. Crimp said Mark had to get his ball himself. "It's a ball now but later on it will be something more important," he explained. "You don't want your parents to be fighting your battles for you."

"Just this once," said Mark. "He's really awfully much bigger."

"I'll help," said John.

"Alone," said Mr. Crimp.

"I'll just cheer him on," said John.

"Get cracking," said Mr. Crimp, like a general. He watched from the window as Mark and John went off. "Good for him," said Mr. Crimp.

"I hope so," said Mrs.

"I'm going too," said Kate.

"Now Kate," said her father turning to her, "this is a man's business."

"Women can cheer as well as men," said Kate, running after them.

"Where's Kate?" asked Susan, coming in from the yard with a bucket of mud.

"Take that out of here," yelled Mrs., trying to protect her carpets.

"It's a pie," Susan said sweetly. "It's for Kate. Especially. I'll just go and give it to her I think."

The baby Nicholas didn't care, he was sleeping in his pram. Mrs. and Mr. Crimp went to the kitchen to have a cuppa. Nobody noticed Mad Martin watching from the stairs.

They were gone, all and every one of them. Nobody remembered him. Maybe they thought I was out, he thought. No, they didn't, he thought. They don't care about me. Of course he could have run after them if he'd wanted. He never did like them much, Mark and John. Charlie was the best. Charlie would be back soon and they were going to plan how to build their own barge.

He went back upstairs and sulked around the room and waited. Then he lay down on the bed and waited some more and maybe he fell asleep because there came a sort of blankness and through it, hazily, the sound of doors opening and closing and the rumble of voices but it was like he was in a molasses jar and couldn't unstick his eyes or unglue his ears.

Then he was wide awake. The house was quiet. Quiet and big and full of something going on. He felt like a ghost, hiding upstairs.

As silently as any ghost, Mad Martin crept down and what he saw was terrible.

They were all of them in the front room, sitting together and drinking tea and eating biscuits which meant it must be a momentous occasion because Mrs. never allowed food in the front room. Mark had his ball back and John was telling how brave he'd been. Mr. Crimp was looking proud and Mrs. was beaming. Kate was agreeing and Susan was cramming biscuits into her mouth. But worst of all, there was Charlie. Charlie was with them instead of with Mad Martin planning how to build the barge and they were all having a party and Mad Martin had not been invited.

But it wasn't only that. It was what he saw happening. Together, all of them, they were what is called a family. Mad Martin was not a Crimp and never would be. He could only pretend to be part of the Crimp family. He would always be on the outside looking in. Before long, he would go away altogether and that would be the end of it.

It wasn't their fault. They couldn't help it if they were related to each other. It made them a family. In a family you could be bad sometimes and good sometimes and do things to be proud of and get love in return. You could even get love when you did things not to be proud of. Because that was the way of families. And in a family you learned all the things of the world and life, you just couldn't help learning because everyone talked all the time.

A grandfather was not a family. A grandfather who never talked couldn't teach you all the different ways of feeling.

Seeing them as he had never seen them before, so clearly united, Mad Martin gave up the hate. Hate was useless, it got you nowhere, in fact it encouraged school rots to kick harder. It would make him ugly, like Charlie said. The ugly would show and not make a good impression, like Mrs. said.

He gave up the hate and he had never found the love. He could watch Crimps loving each other but he couldn't find the feeling in himself. He stood apart, like the ghost he felt he was, and wished he was squashed out of his body and up in people's heaven so that he wouldn't be such a nobody body walking around in a world where everyone was feeling things he couldn't.

The best thing, he thought, is to throw myself in the canal.

"There's Martin," said Mrs. "Come in, Martin, we thought you were having a sleep."

"Mark had a fight," said Kate, making room and wanting him to sit down next to her. "I'll tell you all about it."

"I can tell myself," said Mark.

"Let Kate tell, she tells better," said Susan. They were off arguing again. Mad Martin sat and watched and listened but it was like a blanket had covered him up inside.

At last Charlie was fed up listening to the story of the

famous fight for the twentieth time. "Let's go," he whispered to Mad Martin. "Let's do our plans for the barge."

"Okay," said Mad Martin. But he thought he probably wouldn't be around to see it finished. He would be long gone by then. One way or another.

Chapter 10

🐚〰〰〰〰〰 The Bad Time came back. Giving up hate had left a gaping hole and the Bad Time came swarming in.

He knew it when he woke up one morning too early. He opened his eyes and everything familiar suddenly tilted sideways. Just looking at the chest of drawers and beds and rugs made him feel ill.

When he got up, his legs did their tricks on him. He could feel them one minute and the next they had disappeared so that it was like walking with two chimney stacks instead of legs. He lurched around the floor and there was a thick glassy substance in the air. He had to push at it to get through.

When the Bad Time came, nice things turned sour. Everything he did was spoiled by fear. At breakfast Mrs. tipped a boiled egg into his blue-and-white egg cup. He looked at the egg and thought how good it was going to taste and then, bang, there was this fear thing getting in the way, like bad things would surely happen once the egg was eaten and gone. Enjoyment of eggs was diminished by hopelessness. Nothing seemed to matter. What could matter? They might just as well get squashed and be off to people's heaven.

He felt better if he sat with his arms wrapped around

himself and his legs drawn up. When he could feel himself holding on to himself, he knew he would stay in one place, not go off into a blankness or float up toward the ceiling or do something he didn't know he was doing.

But you couldn't sit that way interminably, it led to suspicion. Mrs. felt his forehead for a fever. Charlie thought he was in the sulks. Kate said he needed to learn a new game. It all made him more nervous than ever and he wished they would go away and stop disturbing the air around him. They made waves in the air and the waves swamped his brain and gave him shudders.

He felt like a bug buried in a ton of cotton. Sinking, lower and lower, down down. Then he had to make a noise, get some air, prove that he was still inside himself and hadn't left himself behind.

Mrs. said she would get a doctor. With great effort, Mad Martin made himself get up and start acting halfway usual.

"I had a stomachache," he explained.

"Well why didn't you say so?" said Mrs. "Too many sweets," she diagnosed. But Mrs. ate far more sweets than any of them and never had a stomachache. He wondered why she believed it.

He went through all the actions of living at Crimps but it was only his body doing it. Deep inside, Mad Martin was alone and terrified.

Then one day the terror went away and he was nothing. He thought someone must have put a machine inside him to pretend that it was Mad Martin. No more feelings, good or bad. The machine did all the work. It didn't have to bother to feel. Soon he would have to tell the machine to take him to the canal and dump him in.

Instead of coming home to Crimps immediately after

school, Mad Martin began going to the house on Mop Street, where he would sit for a few hours in the cold dark front room. Not wanting to arouse any more suspicions, he told Mrs. they were rehearsing a play in school. He planned to let her think he was in it but Mrs. got so excited, saying they would all come to watch, that he had to change it around and say he was only in charge of pulling the curtain.

"Well somebody has to do it," said Mrs., enthusiasm dampened. "Try not to be too late or you'll be caught in the rush."

So every afternoon when Mrs. imagined he was behind the stage, pulling the curtain, Mad Martin was in Mop Street, doing nothing.

Except for what started going on inside his head.

Sort of like dreams. Like having dreams when he was wide awake.

He would sit in the chair in the front room but he wouldn't turn the fire on because he knew it would make the electricity bill higher than it should be with nobody there. Then his grandfather would be cross because he often got cross when he had to spend money. He would be very cross to find out he hadn't saved any electricity by being away in hospital.

Anway, he sat in the chair and got in a blank and then these dreams would start, small bits at first, disconnected and unfathomable.

He dreamed he was in bed with the blankets over his face and a familiar voice was calling him. He peeped out of the blankets and made a sound. The voice called again. And again he peeped out. It was a game of hide and seek. The voice calling to him was like his grandfather's voice.

He liked this dream. It was nice and soothing.

But there was another one that came. This was also about being in bed. He was asleep, and then he would wake up and hear a noise. A big animal was growling outside the bedroom door. It growled and growled, stopped, then growled again. He screamed. His grandfather hurried in. "I was snoring," said his grandfather in the dream, "not growling."

This was a frightening dream until the end when everything turned out all right.

The dream he liked best was the one where they were in a vast park and his grandfather carried a basket with a white cloth over the top and Mad Martin knew without looking that there were good things to eat inside. They watched animals in cages and his grandfather was telling a lion to roar and Mad Martin was laughing.

This was an especially nice dream. He thought it was probably a dream about visiting what was called a Zoo. Too bad it was only a dream. It would have been nice to visit a zoo.

The dreams came all by themselves, without any effort on Mad Martin's part. They would repeat themselves over and over until it was time for him to go back to Crimps. Sometimes, he could even have the dreams at Crimps but it was not quite the same. But if he felt particularly empty, if he felt he was feeling the nothing-feeling especially bad, then he would think up one of these dreams and feel a bit better.

"You're looking happier," Mrs. remarked. "Pulling that curtain must be doing you good."

Yes, it was quite all right for a while. He sat in the cold front room and dreamed the dreams. It was restful. Even the machine inside him needed a rest sometimes.

Then one day, without warning, these nice comfortable familiar dreams changed. All of a sudden out of nowhere came a new one. About a lady.

A lady was sitting in the front room in one of the chairs. She had plump legs and shiny black shoes. She was taking packages out of a shopping bag and handing them to him and his grandfather. Then she put an apron on and went into the kitchen where she opened the oven door and looked inside. A huge joint of meat was spluttering and spitting grease in a roasting pan. Mad Martin was looking at it in the dream but he felt smaller, low down and near the floor. The hissing and crackling made him run away. This shouldn't have been a frightening dream. There was nothing frightening about a roast cooking in an oven. Mrs. had a roast every Sunday and it certainly didn't scare him. No, what he didn't like was the look of that pan the meat was roasting in. It seemed too familiar. It seemed to him that the exact same pan was outside in their own backyard not too long ago. It had dirt in it, and little plants taking root. Then there had been an unexpected frost and the little seedlings died. His grandfather had been more than usually cross then. He had taken the pan, dirt and plants and all, and heaved it into the dustbin. Come to think of it, maybe his grandfather hadn't just been cross. Maybe he had been sad.

I don't think I want to have that dream again, Mad Martin decided. And he didn't. Instead he had another one, even worse.

This time it was another lady, one with thinner legs and brown boots, who trod on one of his toy cars and squashed it. He made a big lot of noise about that, yelling and crying until he was sent to bed. He could hear them talking downstairs, the lady and his grandfather. Their voices made a rumbling sound through the floor and he wished he could know what they were saying. He got out of bed and pressed his ear to the floor. The rumbles couldn't be deciphered into words. When they suddenly stopped he felt frightened. He watched a spider crawl across the floor toward his nose. He pounced on it and pulled off one of its legs.

Ugh, thought Mad Martin, that's a nasty dream. I won't have that one again either. And right off another dream took its place.

Still another lady, with gray hair in a lump on her head. She was petting his arm and saying something and her breath was warm and windy and he didn't like her much.

He was getting fed up having these dreams about ladies. He didn't think he ever knew any such ladies except that they all did seem somehow vaguely familiar. But he didn't know who they could be. He knew one thing. When he dreamed about them, he felt queer. He felt, almost, as if the hate was in danger of creeping back into his body again.

He decided he'd had enough of these dreams going on like that inside his head uninvited. He stopped going to Mop Street for a few days. Instead he and Charlie drew plans for the barge in the afternoons. It was no good, of course. The barge represented the future and Mad Martin didn't have any. His future was a long tunnel of nothingness. He had to get himself organized, he thought, and think what to do. But it was impossible trying to sort himself out among the Crimps. So he had to return to Mop Street to get a little peace and quiet.

"I have to stay late today," he told them one morning.

"More rehearsals?" Mrs. asked.

"Yes," he replied.

"Your play is taking ever so long to get done with," said Kate.

Charlie gave him a funny look.

So he went back to the house. He sat in the front room. He wondered if the house was haunted and these dreams were the spirits trying to tell him something important. He worried that they might get angry if he didn't understand. He moved his chair closer to the door in case of attack. There was no telling what lost souls or spirits could do if you didn't get their message right.

Then came the worst dream of all. It was this:

It was a clear bright day on Mop Street. Mad Martin was waving goodbye to his grandfather from the doorway of the house. His grandfather was waving back. He looked a different grandfather, all dressed up in a suit and tie, his hair combed and watered down and his face all pink and shiny. A big black taxi was coming along the street with a rumbling whine and it stopped in front of their door. A lady got out of the taxi. He knew her name, Mrs. Petra. She was fancy in a blue dress with a bunch of flowers pinned on her chest. She got out of the taxi and gave his grandfather a kiss on the cheek. In the bright sunlight, her white gloves and large white purse dazzled Mad Martin's eyes. She and his grandfather stood together near the taxi and looked at Mad Martin and smiled.

Suddenly Mad Martin was not waving happily anymore. He was angry. Very terrible angry. He rubbed at his sun-dazzled eyes with his fists and stamped his feet. Behind him, a person, a sitter who had come to the house to look after him for the day, tried to get him to shush. She put her arm around his shoulders. He pushed her away. Down by the taxi, his grandfather and Mrs. Petra watched, the smiles on their faces changing into frowns.

For a moment he thought his grandfather was going to come back. But then they were getting into the taxi, the door was shut. Two faces peered out, his grandfather looking worried, Mrs. Petra looking stern. The taxi started off and they were going, leaving him behind and he was being held tight like a rabbit in a trap, a screaming rabbit. And then. He remembered. How he thought his grandfather was being kidnapped by Mrs. Petra. He remembered how he kicked and bit at the sitter's hands and, paying no attention to the anguished cries of warning, ran into the street after the taxi, running, zooming like a bird train, breath dry in his throat, and just when he was almost there a big bang happened . . . so big that it was not possible to believe in it and yet the only pain he felt was the blankness coming down and swallowing him forever.

Mad Martin understood now. They were not dreams, these visions going on inside his head. They were memories.

All the ladies had been friends of his grandfather, long ago, when they had company coming to the house instead of just being alone together. And it seemed like Mad Martin always managed to make a fuss, to do something to make these ladies annoyed which then made his grandfather cross although he couldn't understand why, not at the time. Mrs. Petra was the lady his grandfather was going to marry. Mrs. Petra had put up with all the fusses and not got annoyed and Mad Martin had got used to her but on that day, the day they were going off in the taxi to get married, he realized he didn't want her. Didn't want her coming back to the house and living there with them permanently-like. His grandfather told him how nice it was going to be but Mad

Martin knew it was a trick. All the time he had been getting used to Mrs. Petra, she had been planning this trick. He had wanted to grab the taxi and make it stop.

Instead he had made an accident, the biggest fuss of all. And instead of going to their wedding, they had to take him to hospital. Even Mrs. Petra could not put up with that.

That was the end of the ladies, no more ever came. It was like his grandfather had closed the door and never opened it again. And a big silence settled over everything, smothering talking and laughing forever.

Chapter 11

〰〰〰〰〰 Jump in the canal. He was thinking of doing it. Charlie was wrong about love being for dogs, cars or making babies. Everyone had love all the time. Crimps loved each other because they were a family. His grandfather had loved Mrs. Petra. Maybe people had love when they got up to give old ladies a seat on the bus. Love was all kinds of everythings in all kinds of ways and everybody was probably feeling it at one time or another. Everyone that is except him.

He didn't have any. He had thought, when he went home that afternoon after the terrible memory, that he would try and see if he could fill up the hole the hate had left. Fill it up with love. He looked at the plans for the barge and thought, I'll love the barge, but it didn't work.

He thought if anything he should love the Crimps but he couldn't get any burning feeling inside. Crimps was Crimps and they had all their love tied up with a lot of family strings and ropes and Mad Martin couldn't untie the knots and get himself roped in. He liked them. Well, at least he knew he didn't hate them.

He had no time to wait for a dog. What if he got the dog and he still didn't get the love? That would be too awful, he didn't want to find out. Best thing would be to go back down in the water where he could breathe and feel fine and not be afraid when the drowning took place.

He would leave a note to warn others about such an affliction and he would ask them to finish up his diary by writing: "I died." He was thinking to do it that very day but he went to school first. Not that he was afraid or anything but he wanted some time to get ready. It would be like saying goodbye and he would leave all his books neatly inside his desk.

Right off, he got tripped on the stairs. He said nothing, just gave a small smile. He thought they would feel bad tomorrow when they found out. That would be their punishment for all the kicks and trip-ups he had endured. They would feel bad and perhaps not do it to someone else. He didn't hate them, he felt sorry for them. What kind of life was it when all the fun you got was from tripping people up?

He sat in class like his usual quiet old self. He paid attention and answered the questions and wrote in his book because if you were going to do a noble deed, you shouldn't go around advertising.

When it came time for dinner, he took his smelly cabbage and his horrible soggy pud and ate them all. He felt sorry for the cooks who didn't know how everyone maligned their cooking. He wondered if he should write them a note and tell them to try to improve.

He stood under the leaves of his large bush at recess and wished it goodbye. The bush had, in its own way, been very helpful. He watched all the boys playing in the yard and thought it wasn't their fault. He had acted odd and, as Kate said, people didn't like oddness. They thought you a snob if you didn't know how to play games and didn't talk. People wanted you to be the same as they were. If you weren't, it upset them and they had to kick and punch. You had to talk so you could show you had love.

He had no love inside, it had got left out. He had made the mess about Mrs. Petra because of having no love inside. He had made his grandfather become sad and silent and now their house was like a mole hole and he couldn't see himself going back to that. Not now that he knew everything. He knew too much and there was only one thing for it.

The afternoon classes came and went and Mad Martin had trouble staying still near the end. Goodbyes could only last so long and then you had to go.

At last he started on his way, unencumbered by books. In his pocket were a sheet of paper and a pencil for the note. He would go to the house on Mop Street for one more final time. Look it over and say Zbògom and leave the note on the mantel over the electric fire where they would be sure to find it sooner or later. It was no good writing a note and getting drowned with it, the writing would get all smeary.

He didn't have to even look to find the way home, he knew it by heart. He was busy thinking about what to say in the note and paying no attention to what was going on around him and he was almost there when he looked up and saw.

There were three of them, leaning against a fence, waiting. Oh he recognized them all right, they were the same ones who had followed him home before. He saw them and felt disappointed. He didn't need a bother now. He closed his eyes, wishing them away but like those bad dreams that turned out to be memories, the boys stayed. They smiled at him, the way he had once smiled at himself in the cloakroom mirror, lips stretched tight over grinning teeth. Not a smile at all.

Greasy Hair was the most horrid, with ears sticking way out through his droopy tangles. He was smoking a fag and making out he was tough. He took a long drag and flicked the dogend away over his shoulder. Mad Martin wished it could have landed in the greasy hair and set it on fire, that would have been a right comedown.

There was a short one with a fat stomach, named Mog, and the other was the stair-kicker with the dripping nose. He was wiping it on his sleeve as he stood there. Mrs. wouldn't think they were making a good impression. Talk about urggy, she'd have them in the washer before they knew what was happening.

I'll just cross over the road, Mad Martin thought, and make out like I don't even notice.

He did cross but they followed, in a swaggering way, kicking at rubbish and keeping their hands in their pockets. One of them whistled. Mog blew a raspberry. "Maaartin," the greasy head called, "Martin Dustbin's gone all swank."

"Very flash," said Mog, and blew another disgusting sound.

Mad Martin ignored them, hurrying toward the turning into Mop Street. It wasn't far. If he made it to the door, they wouldn't try nothing more. Sticks and stones, he reminded himself in a Crimp voice, but names won't harm me. He tried not to appear to be running up the road.

"Mad mad Marty, thinks he's a smarty," they jeered, "but he's just a farty."

He risked a turn around to see and they were coming at him, menacing, looming, like a steamroller, banging hard heels into the pavement. If he ran now that would be a signal and they would chase and catch him. If he stayed they would get him anyway. He tried to summon the courage of Mr. Crimp's words. It did not come. His knees began shaking a lot but his feet had turned into concrete blocks and wouldn't budge.

They were all around him now, jabbing, pushing at him but the concrete blocks held firm and he didn't topple and maybe this was a mistake because the pushes got harder. He closed his eyes. Bang it went on the side of his head and momentarily stars flew in his brain. "Stand up for yourself," he heard Mr. Crimp saying, and then a sharp kick in the shins and he let out an "Owww" which pleased them. "Anybody home?" they laughed sneerily and two more blows knocked on the top of his head. "Knock, knock, who's there?"

"Look at him," said Greasy. "Useless, he is."

Hate might help now, thought Mad Martin. If he could yell some "I hate you's" it might put them off. But the hate had gone and only the empty nothing was left inside. But he did feel afraid. Afraid they would knock him out cold or give him an injury which would prevent him from writing the note and getting to the canal. I am useless, he thought. He just didn't have the right equipment in his blood and bones.

And so he was pushed down, getting thumped on his back and neck, feeling their hot breath on his skin, thinking I only hope it's over soon and doesn't hurt too much so that I'll be able to get to the canal; and then he heard a voice, familiar, crying out.

"Hey you yobbos, what kind of odds?"

There was a sound of desperate scuffling and Mad Martin opened his eyes to find Charlie landing a smash on the jaw of Mog. Mog looked surprised. His fat lips went "OOooof."

"Come on, come on," Charlie was shouting, and moving around so that Mad Martin could get himself up. "Let them have it, mate," he said and barely managed to avoid a sock from Greasy who had recovered from the surprise he shared with Mog.

Suddenly things were going Click, Clack, Zap inside Mad Martin's guts. He was filled with a zinging exuberance. Something full and real and pounding thundered through his dried-up veins and muscles. The nothing exploded out of his ears and he was filled up and burning. He lifted his cowardly arms and started punching.

"The yobs," Charlie said and Mad Martin agreed, full of strength now as he bashed and banged and kicked in all directions, and asked, "What are you doing here?"

"Umph," replied Charlie taking a clop in the nose. "I knew you weren't staying for no bloomin' rehearsals. I thought you'd be hiding out in our secret camp."

"Aaaarrroooow," said Mog, getting it again and this time retiring to the curb where he sat down and put his head between his knees and spoke curses to the gutter.

"That's more like it," said Charlie whose nose had started to bleed. "We'll finish them off now, easy like."

It wasn't exactly easy like but Mad Martin hung in, punching, full of energy that came in buckets until he was aware that Charlie was holding him back.

"That's enough, he's had it." There on the pavement lay Greasy, not looking tough anymore, not looking like he ever wanted to get up. Charlie helped him.

"Who the hell are you?" asked the dripping nose, mournfully.

"His mate, that's who," Charlie said and wrapped his arm around Mad Martin's battered neck and pulled him down the street, both of them stumbling and bumping and walking crazily.

"That'll teach them, hey?" he said, holding Mad Martin

close. "That'll show them not to mess around with us!"

The sun was shining, triumphant. The air was cool and good to breathe. Wounds felt fine and blazing and Mod Street was victorious.

"Ha, Haaaaaa," shouted Charlie to the sky.

Amazing amazing came a feeling bursting, surging through Mad Martin's whole insides. I love you, Charlie, he thought.

And the shell cracked open and he came out, born alive. Martin.

Chapter 12

He was changed. He was no longer usually usual. He had all the everythings inside him now: hate and love and talking and smiling and he could play checkers. And because he was changed, Martin felt fearful of going back to Mop Street where the usually usuals would be there waiting, expecting him to be the same.

He didn't want to go back to old ways with the Bad Times and so many blanks. He wanted to progress, as Mrs. called it. "You've progressed since you've been with us," she told him. "Keep up the good work," she said like Mr. Davies in the nursing home.

He didn't want to go backward and he was afraid the house would make him back into the way he once was. And his grandfather. What would his grandfather make of a new and different grandson? Be cross probably. He wouldn't like it.

With no small amount of trepidation, Martin lived out his last days at Crimps, bothering Mrs. so much she couldn't stand it and had to eat two bars of chocolate in one go to calm her nerves. There was so little time and so much he had to know.

"What do you do if you don't have one of these?" he asked her about the washing machine. Because his grandfather's habit was to swish lumps of clothing around in the sink and hang them out to dry in the sooty yard.

"How does one keep from getting urggy?" he wanted to know.

"You change your vest more often for one thing," said Mrs. "And you can take your washing to the launderette. Goodness, I'm sure there's a launderette near Mop Street."

"Thank you," said Martin and made a mental note to take his washing to the launderette when his grandfather wasn't noticing. The only problem was how to get the money.

"I thought you didn't care about looking clean and nice," said Mrs.

"Oh I do now," said Martin who didn't want to hurt her feelings. Privately, he thought the important thing was knowing about feelings and knowing about talking and having a friend: Charlie. But he could understand that being unurggy could have benefits. Not all people had time to find out what was inside, they took a quick look at the outside and made an opinion. It wouldn't hurt to go to the launderette, seeing as how there was no chance of his grandfather's being talked into a washing machine.

But a friend, that was better than all the clean clothes in the world. Charlie had promised they would still go on with building their barge. He told him how they would find another place for the secret camp because Mop Street would no longer be secret with a grandad in residence. This made Martin start wishing that his grandfather could stay away a little longer. But the day came and it was time to leave Crimps and go home.

Mrs. wanted to deliver him. He had to do a lot of this new talking to convince her not to. Then Charlie wanted to come and that was harder to explain but Mrs. helped out by saying Martin wanted to greet his grandfather alone and private like. Martin was thankful because it was going to be hard enough encountering the usually usuals without Charlie there to remind him of the difference.

They all said goodbye very solemnly, Mark and John shaking hands when Mrs. prodded them, and Kate saying, "It was nice having you," in her stuck-up proper voice, and Susan wanting to give him a mud pie to take along. The baby Nicholas didn't say nothing. Mr. Crimp, who was at his job, had said farewells the night before. Charlie said, "See you," and whispered a secret, "Don't forget," to remind him they were still going to build the barge.

"Goodbye, Martin," said Mrs. in a tearful way and she gave him a huge jar of jam to take home. Then she kissed him which he had learned to tolerate, and he was off.

The sameness was there as he expected. His grandfather dozing in the chair, two sticks propped up next to him. The television blared. His box of junk was under the table.

"Hello," said Martin, feeling all gawky.

His grandfather looked him over. "Well, are you planning to stay awhile? Put down all that baggage, don't stand there."

Martin showed him the jam. His grandfather said, "Eh. Too sweet," and made a face. Martin took it into the kitchen and put it on the shelf. He looked around and saw all the usuals as they had always been. The breadboard with its load of crumbs. The marmalade lumps. The crusty stove. It would take a hard lot of cleaning up to make it look even a little bit like Crimps. He picked a dirty old cloth out of the sink and started scrubbing at the lumps. He thought of all the cleaning things Mrs. kept under her sink.

Bottles of disinfectant and scouring powders and scrub brushes and clean cloths. Under the sink here on Mop Street there was only a mousetrap.

"What are you doing in there?" his grandfather called.

"Nothing," said Martin. "Just something."

There was no reply but after a bit his grandfather came to the kitchen door, leaning on his sticks. "Home five minutes and making changes," he said and Martin felt ashamed to be caught in the act.

"Oh no," he said.

"Never mind," said his grandfather, seeming grouchy. He went away, banging with his sticks on the bare floors.

Martin stood holding the cloth, looking at everything and no longer feeling enthusiastic about cleaning up marmalade lumps. He went up to his room.

The room was even worse. It was bare and drab and filled with old urgginess. It had no nice warm carpets like Charlie's room, no bright-colored curtains, no pictures on the walls. No shelves stuffed with books and gadgets and toys.

Martin sat down on his bed and felt awry.

In a way he was glad to be in his own house again. Glad to have his private place with nobody there to interrupt. But he would miss the gargantuan Crimp suppers and the blue-and-white egg cup that held the egg up so straight. Soon his clothes would grow gray and urggy again. Soon Mrs.'s jam would be gone. Soon he would forget all about ever being away and be the same old Martin again. He could feel the walls of the house getting thicker and stronger, wanting to lock him in.

No, he shouted in his mind. I won't let it happen. The house can't take away all my new feelings no matter how it tries. I won't let it, he thought. But a gloomy doubt came creeping in. And a gloomy grouchiness too. He felt angry with the house and wanted to kick it. But it was easier just to keep on sitting on the bed.

"What are you doing up there?" his grandfather was calling. "Come down."

Martin was startled out of his thoughts. He pushed all the clean clothes Mrs. had given him into his chest and hurried down, a little surprised to have been called. Usually his grandfather forgot all about him and left him alone, never asking what he was doing anywhere.

"Shut that thing off," he was told when he came into the room. "I can't hear myself think with all that blah blah." Martin turned the television off. "That's better," his grandfather said. "Now, sit down."

Martin sat down. They looked at each other. Martin hadn't looked at his grandfather properly before and now he did. Although pale, his grandfather looked healthy; he certainly looked clean. He sat as straight as he could with his poor hip, and his eyes seemed different. They were bright. Interested.

"So. How did you like it there?"

"It was fine," said Martin.

"Good cooking?"

"Yes," said Martin.

"And they treated you good?"

"Yes," said Martin.

His grandfather stared at him with his newly bright eyes. "So, nothing else to report?"

Martin thought a moment. All the weeks at Crimps came surging up in his mind, like a gigantic wave. "No," he said.

They were both of them thoughtful for a moment. Then his grandfather cleared his throat. "Well," he said, "what do you think? It's good to get out in the world, eh? You find out what's going on."

"You do, that's a fact," agreed Martin, overwhelmed by the knowledge of it.

"A hospital's not a bad place," his grandfather said and his eyes drifted far away for a moment, as if he was thinking back. "You get all the news. Meet all kinds of people. Who would have thought you'd meet people in a hospital? Mr. Davies, remember him? He's coming around when he gets out. He said he would look us up."

"Mr. Davies, is he coming here?" Martin asked, incredulous.

"Why not?" His grandfather leaned forward. "What's the matter? Shouldn't we have a visitor once in a while? It's too lonesome all cooped up. Walk, they told me. I have to take a walk every day. Ha." He flourished his two sticks. "What do you say? Want to take your grandpa for a walk now and then? Go to the park and see what's going on?"

Martin nodded.

"You know," his grandfather said, "in the hospital, I learned a few things. People have to do more talking. You and I, we have to do more talking together. Otherwise, how are we going to get to know each other?"

Martin opened his mouth to speak but he couldn't get a word in edgewise.

"Another thing," his grandfather was saying. "You're too quiet. I ask you questions and what do I get for answers? Yes no yes. That's no kind of conversation. A boy like you, he should be making noise. What's the matter? I don't mind a little noise. All the time you're creeping around like a mouse." Those bright eyes fixed Martin with a terrible stare. He thought his grandfather was going to be grouchy and cross again. Angry with him for being a mouse. He didn't like that, Martin didn't. He was no mouse, he wasn't!

"But Grandpa," he ventured cautiously, "it's not only me. You're very quiet too." As soon as he said it he felt scared. He thought his grandfather might pick up the two sticks and give him a hit on the head. But instead his grandfather gave a couple of shakes like a fit was coming on. Except it was no fit. His grandfather was chuckling.

"Yes, yes," he said. "The old grandpa gets lazy and forgets to open his mouth." He sighed. "But no more being lazy. Now," he said, thumping the floor with a stick. "Now we both wake up!"

Martin allowed himself a tentative feeling of cheer. A small bit of the depressing usually usuals drifted away and let a clear spot of happy lightness in. But his grandfather was looking very dour. "Something the matter?" he asked.

"No," said Martin, perplexed.

"Then why can't we have a smile, eh? For a starter."

Martin's tight lips quivered. They pulled and stretched. They flicked shakily over his teeth. They smiled at his grandfather, his whole mouth smiling, his whole face smiling.

"That's more like it," said his grandfather and he smiled back and they sat there smiling across the room at each other until they had to stop, feeling a bit embarrassed.

"So!" said his grandfather fussing with his sticks.

It was better. More usually usuals were blowing out the window. Martin felt more courageous. "Grandpa," he said, "you know those stories?"

"What? What stories?"

"Those stories you told Mr. Davies, would you tell them to me?"

"What do you want to hear stories for?"

"Because," said Martin. "I just do." He would have liked to say how it wasn't fair for a grandfather to tell a stranger stories and not his own grandson but he wasn't as courageous as all that.

"I'll tell you stories," his grandfather said, "when I get a cup of tea brought in here to the broken down grandpa, that's when I'll maybe tell you stories."

"I'll make it," said Martin. "Only we have no tea left," he remembered.

"Yes yes. The lady visitor, the casework lady, she brought groceries." He waved toward the kitchen. Martin went to see.

The marmalade lumps and the crumbs seemed less overpowering now. He thought he could easily clean it all up in no time.

"She stuck her nose in, the blebetuša," he heard his grandfather saying, "she gave everything a look over." He sounded more like the old grandfather, wary of nosy neighbors. But when Martin came back with the tea, he was standing in the middle of the room, leaning on his sticks, giving everything a look over himself. "We could use a carpet," he said, as if he had only just realized there was none there.

While he had been making the tea, Martin was thinking of something he felt he must tell his grandfather. He didn't know how to go about such a thing, he could only manage to blurt it out as he handed over the cup. "I'm sorry," he said, "about Mrs. Petra and everything." It had been on his mind, like a sore tooth, bothering him ever since he'd remembered.

His grandfather looked surprised and almost dropped the tea. "Mrs. Petra?" He looked away, then wiped at his eye as if he had a speck of dirt in it. "Don't be sorry," he said gruffly, "for things you don't understand."

"I do understand now," said Martin. "I think." He hoped it was all right to have mentioned it. He hoped it wouldn't go and spoil everything.

"No," said his grandfather. "Some things we don't understand, never. What happens happens. Maybe for the best."

"But," said Martin.

"No," said his grandfather. "We'll think about tomorrows now. The yesterdays we'll leave in the cupboard with the mice."

I'll ask him about a dog tomorrow, thought Martin, or the next day. It wasn't good to rush things, you couldn't do everything at once. Look at how long it took to get hate and love.

He snuggled up in the chair with his cup of tea and prepared to listen. After a long time getting started, his grandfather began to tell a story.

"When I was a boy," he said, "like your age, I lived on an island. We had a farm but it was very poor, we didn't grow much, mostly rocks. We had some chickens and my sister took the eggs to sell. My sister was busy selling eggs and my mother busy cooking and sewing and my father busy breaking up the rocks. I was busy doing nothing. One day I found a goat. A small goat. I thought, I haven't got anything to do so I will be a friend with the goat. I waited until night and brought him home and put him under the blankets of my bed so my mother wouldn't catch me. But a goat doesn't want to sleep under blankets. All it wants to do is eat and be a goat. The goat ate a hole in the blankets and stuck out his head. What's this? my mother asked. This is my friend, I told her. There is your friend, she said and put him out the door. I was crying. Why do you cry? she asked me. Because my friend is outside, cold and alone. My mother laughed. You are the one who is cold, she said, covered by a blanket full of holes. As for alone, the goat is happy being with other goats. A person is happy with other people. Here are we, she said, and while you may be cold you are not alone. Now decide what you want to be, a boy or a goat, you can't be both."

Martin listened and knew these were stories about yesterdays but it was all right to think of them because they were yesterdays of long ago. Someday the yesterday of Mrs. Petra would be long ago and maybe they would talk about it.

"It's a funny thing," his grandfather said. "My mother told me that a person is happy with other people and I had forgotten it. Not until I fell down the stairs and broke my hip did I remember it again. And that's why I say, what happens happens, maybe for the best."

Martin was sad and glad. Glad and sad. He sat on the floor and pushed the junk around for a while and then put everything back in its box under the table. His grandfather snoozed in the chair. The electric fire glowed. Tomorrow they would go for a walk and maybe they would buy a carpet. He would clean the kitchen and make it shining for when Mr. Davies would come.

He took out his diary and turned to the last remaining

page. He wrote: "I am home. It is nice to come home. It is not going to be the same sameness ever again and we are going to have a carpet and a visitor. Charlie and I are going to build the barge. This diary is finished. Tomorrow I'll start a new one. But for now, this is The End."